情境會話 × 萬用好句 × 生活單字

山田社
San Tian She

遊學、留學生活英語
一個月就出發去歐美

李洋 著

U0080333

打工度假近來正夯，
到國外去蹓躂一下，
可說是大家躍躍欲試的夯選項喔！

你是不是把學習想太難了？

★ **親朋好友的話題？**

　　最近是否常聽到這樣的話題：「我暑假打算到波士頓遊學3個月」、「我妹妹想到澳洲打工6個月」、「我女兒想到日本遊學1年」。

★ **打工度假跟「遊學」有何不同？**

　　的確，很多人都嚮往在國外遊學，一邊工作、一邊旅行。一邊在全英文的環境下工作，每天用每天聽，英文進步絕對很大。另外，一邊看遍國外美景，感受當地的人文生活，認識來自世界各地的人，各式各樣嶄新的體驗讓人獲益良多。

★ **學習語言跟「老師」及「教材」有什麼關係？**

　　出國不再遙不可及，本書專為嚮往出國遊學或留學生活的您，量身打造您的遊學·留學夢，內容有：

● 食衣住行輕鬆開口説

● 老外都在用的談天、交友好用句

LET'S GO!

●怎麼跟鄰居打招呼

●從到國外旅行，就開始喜歡英文…等。

　　有了好的英語基礎，再透過遊學・留學的洗禮，不需要名校的光環，就可以幫助您拿到出色的英語證書了。

★ 本書提供哪些想學好英語的你什麼？

　　《遊學・留學生活英語—— 一個月就出發去歐美》不論打工遊學、短長期遊學、交換學生、背包客、一般旅遊都適用。跟著我們學好英語，幫你創造非典型的歐美生活體驗！

★ 覺得自己基礎不好的朋友別擔心，在歐美獨立生活不是問題！

　　本書有54個實用生活會話，500句以上萬用好句，超過600個生活單字。只要靈活替換生活單字，句子應用就加倍加倍再加倍！所有的生活場景都難不倒你，仿佛身歷其境，不怕溝通障礙，讓你找工作、學習、旅行、交友更省時省力。

目錄
CONTENT

Chapter **1** 社交一下

1	日常的招呼	8
2	自我介紹	12
3	介紹他人	16
4	再見	20
5	道歉	24
6	感謝	28
7	讚美‧安慰	32
8	贊成‧反對	36
9	祝賀‧應和	40
10	請求	44

Chapter **2** 找話題聊天

1	天氣	50
2	學校	54
3	興趣	58
4	電視	62
5	流行	66
6	食物	70
7	旅行	74
8	運動	78
9	寵物	82
10	算命	86
11	風俗習慣	90

Chapter **3**
拜訪老外

1	打電話	96
2	接電話	100
3	打錯電話	104
4	約時間	108
5	帶到家裡	112
6	進入老外的家	116
7	介紹家人及其他客人	120
8	一起進餐	124
9	找聊天對象	128
10	聊天技巧	132
11	告辭	136

Chapter **4**
輕鬆生活・旅遊

1	找房子・工作	142
2	超市	146
3	百貨公司	150
4	銀行	154
5	郵局	158
6	餐廳	162
7	帶到桌子	166
8	點餐	170
9	付帳	174
10	購物	178
11	購物 II	182
12	觀光服務站	186
13	遊覽	190
14	買票	194

目錄

CONTENT

Chapter 5
一路通的交通

1　問路 ………………………………… 200
2　怎麼坐車還有租車呢？ ………… 204
3　電車 ………………………………… 208
4　地鐵 ………………………………… 212
5　公車 ………………………………… 216
6　計程車 ……………………………… 220

Chapter 6
緊急應變

1　發生緊急情況 ……………………… 224
2　生病了 ……………………………… 228

Chapter 1 社交一下

Unit 1 ★ 日常的招呼

1

Good <u>morning</u>!
早安！

Good evening, sir.
晚安！先生。

Good luck!
祝你好運！

 替換看看

afternoon 下午	evening 傍晚，晚上
night 晚上	morning 早上
day （一）天；白天	to see you 見到你

2 How is <u>everything</u>?

一切都還好嗎？

How is Mary?

瑪莉還好嗎？

How is it going?

（近況）還好嗎？

 換個單字意思就不一樣囉 ◆◆◆

it going	your family
近況	你家人

work	your wife
工作	尊夫人

school	the new teacher
學校	新老師

怎樣都要知道的句子

1. 可以這樣說 1-2.

- Good morning!
  早安！

- How are you today?
  你今天好嗎？

- How is your family?
  你家人好嗎？

- How is everything?
  一切都還好嗎？

- What's up?
  怎麼樣呢？

2. 也可以這樣說

- I'm fine, thank you.
  我很好，謝謝你！

- Not bad. How about you?
  還不錯，你呢？

- I'm great! Thank you!
  我很好！謝謝你！

- So far, so good.
  目前為止，都還好！

- Nice day, isn't it?
  天氣不錯吧！

1-3

A：Hi, Mary.

B：Hi, Tom. How is everything?

A：Pretty good. How about you?

B：Well, busy, but fine.

A：Take care of yourself, OK?

A：嗨，瑪麗。

B：嗨，湯姆。一切都還好嗎？

A：還不賴，妳呢？

B：這個嘛，忙，不過還好。

A：要照顧好自己，好嗎？

你 一 定 會 用 的 句 型　 1-4

1

My name is <u>John Jones</u>.

我的名字是<u>約翰瓊斯</u>。

My name is Ian.

我的名字是伊恩。

My name is Tom.

我的名字是湯姆。

◆◆◆ 替換看看 ◆◆◆

Meiling Chen 陳美玲	Ming Wu 吳明
Keiko Suzuki 鈴木惠子	David Shultz 大衛舒茲
Denzel Washington 丹佐華盛頓	James Bond 詹姆士龐德

2 I'm from <u>Canada</u>.
我來自加拿大。

She is from Australia.
她來自澳洲。

Her family is from Europe.
她的家族是從歐洲來的。

 換個單字意思就不一樣囉

Taiwan 台灣	China 中國
the U.S.A 美國	Japan 日本
Canada 加拿大	Korea 韓國

怎樣都要知道的句子

1. 可以這樣説 1-5

- Excuse me. May I talk to you?
  不好意思，我可以跟你說話嗎？

- May I introduce myself?
  可以讓我自我介紹一下嗎？

- My name is George.
  我的名字是喬治。

- I'm from Canada.
  我來自加拿大。

- I'm a student.
  我是個學生。

2. 也可以這樣説

- I'm 20 years old.
  我20歲。

- I'm a Libra.
  我是天秤座。

- I live in Taipei.
  我住在台北。

- I live with my family.
  我跟家人住。

- I work for a big company.
  我在一家大公司上班。

A：Hi! My name is Jane.

B：Nice to meet you, Jane. I'm

Linda.

A：Nice to meet you, too.

B：Where are you from?

A：I am from Taiwan.

A：嗨！我的名字是珍。

B：很高興認識妳，珍。我是
琳達。

A：我也很高興認識妳。

B：妳是哪裡人？

A：我是台灣來的。

Unit 3 ★ 介紹他人

1 This is my <u>wife</u>.
這位是我太太。

This is my book.
這是我的書。

This is my bike.
這是我的腳踏車。

◆◆◆ 替換看看 ◆◆◆

mother 媽媽	wife 妻子	husband 丈夫
uncle 叔叔、舅舅	aunt 姨媽、姑姑	cousin 表兄弟姐妹
niece 姪女、外甥女	nephew 姪子、外甥	son 兒子
daughter 女兒	boyfriend 男朋友	fiancé 未婚夫（妻）

2 My father is a/an <u>journalist</u>.

我父親是一位<u>記者</u>。

That is a hotel.

那是一家飯店。

This is a new mobile phone.

這是支新的手機。

 ◆◆◆ 換個單字意思就不一樣囉 ◆◆◆

doctor 醫生	nurse 護士	businessperson 商人
writer 作家	reporter 記者	student 學生
fashion designer 服裝設計師	teacher 老師	police officer 警察
lawyer 律師		

怎樣都要知道的句子

■ Let me introduce you to my son, John.
讓我來跟你介紹一下，這是我兒子約翰。

■ This is Mary.
這是瑪莉。

■ Jeff, this is Ana. Ana, this is Jeff.
傑夫，這位是安娜，安娜，這位是傑夫。

■ Nice to meet you.
很高興認識你。

■ **I am Frank. It's so nice to meet you.**
我是法蘭克，真的很高興認識你。

2. 也可以這樣說

■ He is from Chicago.
他來自芝加哥。

■ Have you met already?
你們見過面了嗎？

■ I'd like to meet your wife.
我很高興能見到您夫人。

■ I think you'll be good friends.
我覺得你們可以成為好朋友。

■ We often talk to each other.
我們經常聊天。

1-9

A：Tom, this is my wife, Mary.

B：Hello, Mary. Nice to meet you.

C：Hi, Tom! I am glad to meet you, too.

A：Tom's a lawyer.

C：I know. Tom, he has told me a lot about you.

A：湯姆，這是我太太瑪麗。

B：嗨！瑪麗，很高興認識妳。

C：嗨，湯姆！我也很高興認識你。

A：湯姆是律師。

C：我知道。湯姆，他跟我說了好多你的事情呢！

Unit 4 ★ 再見

你一定會用的句型  1-10

1

See you <u>tomorrow</u>.
明天見。

See you there.
那裡見。

See you around.
隨後見。

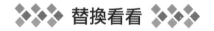
替換看看

next Monday 下星期一	next year 明年
later 晚點	next time 下一次
soon 很快	again 再次

2 Have a <u>nice weekend</u>!
祝你有個美好的週末！

Have a wonderful time.
祝你玩得愉快。

Have a great date.
祝你有個美好的約會。

 換個單字意思就不一樣囉

nice flight 愉快的飛行	nice trip 愉快的旅途
nice voyage 愉快的航行	wonderful vacation 美好的假期
pleasant flight 愉快的飛航	good day 美好的一天

怎樣都要知道的句子

1. 可以這樣說 1-11

■ How have you been?
最近可好？

■ I've been fine, thank you. And you?
我很好。謝謝你！你呢？

■ I've been fine, too. Thank you.
我也很好。謝謝你！

■ What a surprise to see you!
能跟你碰面真叫人意外啊！

■ Good bye!
再見！

2. 也可以這樣說

■ Take care!
路上小心！

■ Have a nice weekend!
祝你有個快樂的週末！

■ Good luck.
祝你好運！

■ Bye-bye. Don't work too hard.
再見！工作不要太辛苦了。

■ Say hello to your wife for me.
請代我向尊夫人問好。

 1-12

A：I have to go now.

B：Okay, Say hello to your family for me.

A：I sure will. See you next time.

B：Good luck!

A：我現在得走了。

B：好的！請代我向你家人問好。

A：我會的。下回見。

B：祝你好運！

Unit 5 ★ 道歉

你一定會用的句型  1-13

1

I'm <u>sorry</u>.
我很抱歉。

I'm busy.
我很忙。

I'm poor, but I'm happy.
我很窮，但我很開心。

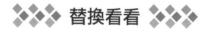 替換看看

so sorry 非常抱歉	very sorry 很抱歉
really sorry 真的很抱歉	surprised 很驚訝
fine 很好	not sure 不確定

24

2 I didn't <u>mean it</u>.
我不是（沒）故意的。

I didn't order this.
我沒有點這個。

I didn't want to bother you.
那時候我並沒有打擾你的意思。

 換個單字意思就不一樣囉

mean to do it 故意那樣做的	mean to do that 故意那樣做的
mean to say that 故意那樣說的	know 知道
order this 叫這個	hear it 聽到

怎樣都要知道的句子

1. 可以這樣説  1-14

- Excuse me.
  對不起。

- It's my fault.
  那是我的錯。

- Please forgive me.
  請原諒我。

- I apologize for troubling you.
  很抱歉讓你這麼麻煩。

- Oops! My mistake!
  唉呦！是我的錯！

2. 也可以這樣説

- Sorry I'm late.
  抱歉我遲到了。

- Sorry I didn't call.
  抱歉我沒打電話過去。

- Sorry for lying.
  抱歉我説了謊。

- That's OK. Don't worry.
  沒關係，別擔心。

- I was wrong, too.
  我也有錯。

超常用對話

CD 1-15

A：I have something to tell you,

　　Ann.

B：What is it?

A：I lost your book. I'm sorry.

B：Oh, that's OK.

A：安，我有事情要告訴妳。

B：是什麼事？

A：我把妳的書弄丟了，我很
　　抱歉。

B：喔，沒關係的。

Unit 6 ★ 感謝

你一定會用的句型  1-16

1

Thank you <u>very much</u>.
感謝你<u>萬分</u>。

Thank you for seeing me.
謝謝你見我。

Thank you for the gift.
謝謝你的禮物。

 替換看看

so much 萬分	for your help 你的幫助
for all you've done 你所做的	for everything 你的多方關照
for coming 你能來	for your kindness 你的親切

2 I had a <u>nice</u> time.
我度過了一段美好的時光。

You have a bigger car.
你有一個大車子。

You have a small house.
你有一個小房子。

◆◆◆ 換個單字意思就不一樣囉 ◆◆◆

lovely
可愛的

swell
極好的

great
很棒的

wonderful
美妙的

good
好的

happy
快樂的

怎樣都要知道的句子

- Thank you for everything.
  謝謝你各方面的關照。

- I enjoyed the movie.
  我很喜歡這齣電影。

- I appreciate your love.
  我很感謝你對我的愛。

- That's just perfect!
  那太完美了。

- I like it very much.
  我很喜歡它。

2. 也可以這樣說

- You're welcome.
  不客氣。

- My pleasure.
  我很榮幸。

- It was my pleasure.
  那是我的榮幸。

- Not at all.
  不客氣。

- Don't mention it.
  快別那麼說了。

1-18

A：I can't find my pen. May I
use yours?

B：Yes. Here you are.

A：Thank you for your kindness.

B：Not at all.

A：我找不到我的原子筆。我
可以用你的嗎？

B：好啊，拿去。

A：謝謝你這麼好。

B：不客氣。

你一定會用的句型  1-19

1 That's <u>great</u>.
那真是太好了。

That's great news.
那真是好消息。

That's pretty cool.
那滿酷的。

◆◆◆ 替換看看 ◆◆◆

good 好	wonderful 太棒了
nice 好	interesting 有趣了
amazing 了不起	a good idea 一個好主意

2 Give it <u>a try</u>.
試試看吧。

Give me a minute.
給我一分鐘。

Give me a chance.
給我一個機會。

 換個單字意思就不一樣囉

a shot
試試看

your best shot
好好試試看

your best
盡你最大的能力

the old college try
盡你最大的能力

another shot
再試一次

one last try
再試最後一次

怎樣都要知道的句子

 1-20

1. 可以這樣說

- That's great!
  那很棒！

- Good job!
  做得好！

- You did it!
  你做到了！

- You look nice.
  你看起來氣色很好！

- I envy you.
  我很嫉妒你。

2. 也可以這樣說

- I'm sorry to hear that.
  聽到那事我覺得很難過。

- It's not your fault.
  那不是你的錯。

- Cheer up!
  打起精神來！

- Don't worry. I'm here.
  別擔心！我會在你身旁的。

- Everything will be fine.
  一切都會好轉的。

CD 1-21

A：I am getting married.

B：Congratulations! What's your wife like?

A：Well, she's a good cook.

B：That's terrific.

A：But she's not good at remembering things.

B：Oh! It'll be all right.

A：我要結婚了。

B：恭喜！你太太人怎麼樣？

A：這個嘛，她是個烹飪高手。

B：那很棒啊！

A：不過她的記性不太好。

B：是喔？她會變好的啦！

Unit 8 ★ 贊成・反對

你一定會用的句型  1-22

1

That's <u>true</u>.
那倒是真的。

That's a wonderful idea.
你這個主意挺絕的。

That's a good question.
你這問題問得好。

◆◆◆ 替換看看 ◆◆◆

right 對的	interesting 有趣的
fine with me 可以的	a good one 好的
a great idea 很棒的點子	possible 可能

2 You're <u>wrong</u>.

你錯了。

You're hopeless!

你沒救了！

You're crazy.

你瘋了。

 換個單字意思就不一樣囉 ◆◆◆

off
錯了

dead wrong
錯得離譜了

way off base
大錯特錯了

missing the boat
錯失良機

absolutely wrong
完全錯了

lying through
your teeth
謊話連篇

怎樣都要知道的句子

1. 可以這樣說  1-23

- I agree.
  我同意。

- Yes, I think so too.
  對的，我也這麼認為。

- I think you're right.
  我認為你是對的。

- Sounds good.
  聽起來很不賴啊！

- I'm in.
  我加入。

2. 也可以這樣說

- I don't agree.
  我不同意。

- That's impossible.
  那不可能的。

- I don't think so.
  我不這麼認為。

- You're wrong.
  你錯了。

- Please think it over.
  請重新考慮一下。

1-24

A：That's a wonderful idea.

B：I'm sorry, but I don't think so.

A：I think it's time-saving.

B：Well, that's true.

A：那點子很棒。

B：抱歉，但我不這麼覺得。

A：我覺得它很省時的。

B：嗯！那倒是真的。

Unit 9 ★ 祝賀・應和

你一定會用的句型  1-25

1

Happy <u>birthday</u>!
生日快樂！

Happy New Year!
新年快樂！

Merry Christmas!
聖誕節快樂！

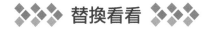 替換看看

Anniversary 週年紀念	Halloween 萬聖節前夕
Valentine's Day 情人節	Father's Day 父親節
Mother's Day 母親節	Thanksgiving 感恩節

2 I wish you <u>happiness</u>!
我祝你<u>快樂</u>！

I wish you all the best.
我祝你一切都好。

I wish you luck.
我祝你好運。

 換個單字意思就不一樣囉 ◆◆◆

success	good luck
成功	幸運

good health	the best of everything
健康	一切順利

good luck in your work	a Merry Xmas and a Happy New Year
工作幸運	聖誕快樂跟新年快樂

怎樣都要知道的句子

1. 可以這樣說 1-26

- Congratulations!
  恭喜！

- Happy birthday!
  生日快樂！

- You must be happy.
  你一定很快樂！

- You finally did it.
  你終於做到了！

- Wow! That's wonderful!
  哇！那真是太棒了！

2. 也可以這樣說

- I see.
  我瞭解。

- Really?
  真的嗎？

- Unbelievable!
  真不敢相信！

- I guess so.
  我猜是這樣吧。

- No wonder.
  難怪。

CD 1-27

A：Happy birthday, Mary! This is for you.

B：Oh, thank you. Can I open it?

A：Sure. Go ahead.

B：Oh, This is just what I've wanted. Thank you so much.

A：You're welcome. I'm glad you like it.

A：生日快樂！瑪莉！這送給妳。

B：喔！謝謝你！我可以打開嗎？

A：可以啊，打開看看。

B：哇！這正是我一直想要的，太謝謝你了。

A：不客氣。我很高興妳喜歡。

Unit 10 ★ 請求

你一定會用的句型  1-28

1

Could you please <u>speak slower</u>?
可以請你說慢一點嗎？

Could you please keep quiet?
可以請你保持安靜嗎？

Could you please bring me a glass of water?
可以請你拿一杯水給我嗎？

◆◆◆ 替換看看 ◆◆◆

speak louder 說大聲一點	write it down 把它寫下來
spell that 拼出那個字	tell me the time 告訴我時間
stop doing that 別再那麼做了	leave me alone 別管我

2 I'd like to <u>send a postcard</u>.

我想要寄一張明信片。

I'd like to see a timetable.

我想要看時刻表。

I'd like to rent a car.

我想要租一輛車。

 換個單字意思就不一樣囉

see a doctor
看醫生

try skiing
嘗試滑雪

buy a swimsuit
買游泳衣

pay by credit card
刷卡付費

return this
歸還這個

get off here
在這裡下車

怎樣都要知道的句子

1. 可以這樣說

■ Please.
拜託你。

■ Please help me.
請幫助我。

■ May I ask your phone number?
我可以跟你要電話嗎？

■ Would you do it for me?
你可以幫我做嗎？

■ I'm begging you.
我求你。

2. 也可以這樣說

■ Can I keep it?
我可以留著它嗎？

■ I don't understand.
我不懂。

■ No smoking, please.
請不要抽煙。

■ May I try this on?
我可以試穿這件嗎？

■ Shall I open the windows?
要我打開窗戶嗎？

 1-30

A：Look at that bird, Dad.

B：Wow! What a small bird!

　　How cute!

A：Can I keep it?

B：No, Mary, you can't.

A：你看那隻鳥，爸爸。

B：哇！好小的鳥喔！真可愛！

A：我可以把牠帶回去嗎？

B：不，瑪莉，妳不行。

Note

Chapter **2** 找話題聊天

Unit 1 ★ 天氣

你 一 定 會 用 的 句 型   1-31

1

It's <u>hot</u> today.
今天真是<u>熱</u>。

It is snowy outside.
外面在下雪。

It's too cold today.
今天太冷了。

 替換看看

cool 涼快	cold 寒冷
cloudy 多雲	warm 溫暖
windy 多風	rainy 多雨

2 The weather is <u>good</u>.

天氣很<u>好</u>。

The weather was great.

當時天氣很棒。

It was sunny.

當時天氣晴朗。

 換個單字意思就不一樣囉

nice	clear
很好	很晴朗

mild	terrible
很溫和	糟糕

unstable	changeable
很多變	很變化多端

怎樣都要知道的句子

 1-32

1. 可以這樣説

- It's a beautiful day, isn't it?
  天氣真棒,不是嗎?

- It's hot, isn't it?
  天氣真熱,不是嗎?

- It'll be fine tomorrow.
  明天天氣會很好。

- It looks like rain, doesn't it?
  好像會下雨,是不是?

- It's getting a little cold.
  天氣變得有點涼了。

2. 也可以這樣説

- How's the weather there?
  那邊的天氣如何?

- Spring is almost here.
  春天快到了。

- The days are getting longer.
  白天越來越長了。

- It's typhoon season.
  這是多颱的季節。

- It's already winter.
  已是冬天了。

CD 1-33

A：How's the weather outside?

B：It's raining. That's why I'm so wet.

A：Don't you have an umbrella?

B：No, I don't. It was sunny when I left home.

A：外面的天氣怎麼樣啊？

B：正在下雨。這就是為什麼我會這麼濕。

A：你沒帶雨傘嗎？

B：沒有啊，我出門的時候天氣還很晴朗呢！

Unit 2 ★ 學校

1

Our <u>math</u> test is tomorrow.
明天我們有數學考試。

Our meeting is today.
今天有會要開。

Our team is in the playoffs.
我們隊打入複賽了。

 替換看看

history 歷史	music 音樂
art 藝術	English 英文
science 科學	social sciences 社會學

2 We have <u>an hour for lunch</u>.

我們有（要）一小時可以吃午餐。

We have some old books.

我們有一些舊書。

We have many good friends.

我們有很多好朋友。

 換個單字意思就不一樣囉

to keep our hair short 留短髮	to wear a school uniform 穿制服
a big test tomorrow 明天有大考	no school tomorrow 明天不用上課
classes from 8 a.m. to 6 p.m. 從八點上課到六點	a good teacher 一個好老師

怎樣都要知道的句子

1. 可以這樣説

■ I attend classes.
我有去上課。

■ I never cut classes.
我從不蹺課。

■ I have club practice after school.
我下課後去參加社團活動。

■ We have the 6-3-3 educational system.
我們是6-3-3學制的。

■ The school year is from September to July.
從九月到七月是一個學期。

2. 也可以這樣説

■ How's school?
上課還好嗎?

■ I study 6 subjects a day.
我一天上六個科目。

■ I study at the library.
我在圖書館唸書。

■ I hand in my homework.
我交作業。

■ I eat lunch at the school cafeteria.
我在學校餐廳吃午餐。

 1-36

A：There's a math test tomorrow.

B：Oh, I forgot about it.

A：I'm going to study for it in the library this afternoon. Do you want to join me?

B：That's a good idea. See you then.

A：明天有數學考試。

B：噢，我忘了這回事了。

A：今天下午我要去圖書館唸書，準備考試，你要一起來嗎？

B：好主意，到時候見了。

Unit **3** ★ 興趣

你一定會用的句型  1-37

1 My hobby is <u>collecting cards</u>.
我的嗜好是<u>收集卡片</u>。

My hobby is making songs.
我的興趣是創作歌曲。

I like to write my own stories.
我喜歡寫自己的故事。

 替換看看

listening to music 聽音樂	singing karaoke 唱卡拉OK
reading 閱讀	watching TV 看電視
surfing the Internet 上網	playing video games 玩電視遊樂器

2 Do you like <u>classical music</u> ?
你喜歡<u>古典樂</u>嗎？

Do you shop online?
你上網購物嗎？

Do you know her?
你認識她嗎？

 換個單字意思就不一樣囉

popular music 流行樂	jazz 爵士樂
rap 饒舌	symphonic music 交響樂
Punk music 龐克樂	Hip-hop music 嘻哈樂

怎樣都要知道的句子

1. 可以這樣說 1-38

- What are your hobbies?
  你的興趣是什麼？

- Do you like Jazz?
  你喜歡爵士樂嗎？

- I'm interested in Chinese history.
  我對中國歷史很感興趣。

- I like romance novels.
  我喜歡浪漫小說。

- He is a wonderful actor.
  他是一個很棒的演員。

2. 也可以這樣說

- I enjoy reading comic books.
  我很喜歡看漫畫書。

- My favorite movie is "*Titanic*".
  我最喜歡的電影是「凱達尼號」。

- I hardly watch TV.
  我很少看電視。

- I'm not into sports.
  我對運動不感興趣。

- I like being a business salesperson.
  我喜歡當一個業務員。

超常用對話

CD 1-39

A：Do you like sports, Sam?

B：Yes, and I like basketball the best. How about you, Beth?

A：I like skiing. It's fun.

B：Oh, is it?

A：Yeah, I like winter sports.

A：你喜歡運動嗎，山姆？

B：喜歡，而且我最喜歡的是籃球。妳呢，貝絲？

A：我喜歡滑雪，那很有趣呢！

B：喔，是嗎？

A：是啊！我喜歡冬季的運動。

Unit 4 ★ 電視

你一定會用的句型  1-40

1

What's on TV?
電視在播什麼？

What's on the desk?
書桌上的是什麼？

What's the movie about?
電影的主題是什麼？

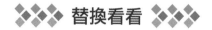

tonight 今晚	the tube 有線電視
Channel Five 第五台	HBO 美國電影台HBO
the Discovery channel 探索頻道	the National Geographic channel 國家地理頻道

2 I like <u>action movies</u>.

我喜歡動作片。

I like Chinese food.
我喜歡中國菜。

I like my brother.
我喜歡我哥哥（弟弟）

◆◆◆ 換個單字意思就不一樣囉 ◆◆◆

romance movies 愛情片	comedies 喜劇
animated movies 動畫	mysteries 懸疑片
horror movies 恐怖片	cartoons 卡通

怎樣都要知道的句子

1. 可以這樣說 1-41

■ Do you watch TV a lot?
你常看電視嗎？

■ I often watch dramas.
我常看連續劇。

■ It's on Channel 74, starting at 9:00 p.m.
它在74頻道，晚上9點開始播放。

■ I recommend it.
我推薦它。

■ Stop switching channels.
不要一直轉台。

2. 也可以這樣說

■ Let's watch the news.
我們來看新聞吧！

■ Do you like American TV shows?
你喜歡看美國電視節目嗎？

■ This show is interesting.
這個節目很有趣。

■ I just watch news programs.
我只看新聞節目。

■ It's waste of time to watch TV.
看電視很浪費時間。

1-42

A：Did you watch the baseball game on TV last night?

B：Yes, of course.

A：How was it?

B：Very exciting! Chin-Yuen Chen hit a home run. He's my favorite.

A：He's a good player.

A：你昨天晚上看了電視轉播的棒球比賽了嗎？

B：當然看了啊！

A：賽況如何？

B：很刺激！陳致遠擊出了一支全壘打。我最喜歡他了。

A：他是個優秀的選手。

Unit 5 ★ 流行

你一定會用的句型  1-43

1

It is <u>in fashion</u>.
它現在是很<u>流行</u>。

It is so cool.
那好酷喔！

This is out of style.
這已經不流行了。

 替換看看

a new fashion 新流行	up to date 最新的
the fad today 最新流行的	trendy 時髦的
out of style 退流行的	out of date 過時的

66

2 I read <u>fashion magazines</u>.

我有看時尚雜誌。

I read newspapers.
我有看報紙。

What kind of magazine do you like to read?
你喜歡看什麼樣的雜誌？

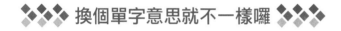 換個單字意思就不一樣囉

Vogue magazine Vogue雜誌	Trend reports 潮流報導
posts on a fashion blog 時尚部落格上的文章	Marie Claire magazine 美麗佳人雜誌
MF (music fashion) magazine MF雜誌	Esquire magazine Esquire 雜誌

怎樣都要知道的句子

1. 可以這樣說  1-44

- That's the latest fashion.
  那是最新的流行。

- I want to look cool.
  我希望看起來很酷。

- I'm fussy about clothing.
  我很講究穿著。

- I love Prada bags.
  我喜歡Prada包包。

- This color will be fashionable this fall.
  這個顏色在秋天會很流行。

2. 也可以這樣說

- This is out dated.
  這已經退流行了。

- The dress is really loud.
  這洋裝太花俏了。

- I'm not a good dresser.
  我不太會穿衣服。

- I look great in this shirt.
  我穿這件襯衫看起來很棒。

- What color will be in this winter?
  哪個顏色在本季的冬天會很流行呢？

CD 1-45

A：You look amazing today, Jane! New skirt?

B：Yes, it is. Miniskirts are in fashion now.

A：Yeah, I've heard.

B：I thought you weren't interested in fashion.

A：Well, I read fashion magazines sometimes.

A：妳今天很漂亮呢，珍！新裙子嗎？

B：是啊，現在迷你裙正在流行呢。

A：嗯，我聽說了。

B：我以為妳對流行沒興趣呢。

A：這個嘛，我有時候會看時尚雜誌啊！

Unit 6 ★ 食物

你一定會用的句型  1-46

Do you like <u>Taiwanese food</u>?
你喜歡台灣食物嗎？

Do you like your job?
你喜歡你的工作嗎？

Do you like music?
你喜歡音樂嗎？

◆◆◆ 替換看看 ◆◆◆

Japanese food 日式菜	Indian food 印度菜
Chinese food 中國菜	Korean food 韓國菜
Italian food 義大利菜	French food 法國菜

2 What kind of <u>beer</u> do you have?
你們有什麼啤酒呢？

What kind of dressing do you have?
你們有什麼醬料呢？

What kind of juice do you have?
你們有什麼果汁呢？

 換個單字意思就不一樣囉

wine 酒	salad 沙拉
dessert 點心	steak 牛排
pizza 比薩	sauce 醬汁

怎樣都要知道的句子

1. 可以這樣説 1-47

- **What's your favorite food?**
  你最喜歡吃什麼食物？

- **This is so yummy!**
  這真好吃！

- **I'll take you to a Chinese restaurant.**
  我會帶你去一家中國餐廳。

- **How's the taste?**
  味道如何？

- **Do you know what it is?**
  你知道這是什麼嗎？

2. 也可以這樣説

- **Let's have a drink this evening.**
  今晚我們去喝一杯吧！

- **What do you drink at dinner?**
  你晚餐喝什麼？

- **Scotch on the rocks, please.**
  麻煩蘇格蘭威士忌酒加冰塊。

- **How about beer?**
  要不要來杯啤酒？

- **I had enough.**
  我不喝了。

CD 1-48

A：This cake looks delicious.

B：I made it, actually.

A：Really? Can I have some?

B：Sure.

A：Umm…what is this?

B：That's Mango.

A：Well, it is very sour!

A：這蛋糕看起來很好吃的樣
　　子。

B：其實這是我做的。

A：真的嗎？我可以吃一點
　　嗎？

B：當然可以啊！

A：我吃吃看...，這是什麼？

B：這是芒果。

A：恩，這好酸喔！

Unit 7 ★ 旅行

你一定會用的句型　CD 1-49

1

I want to <u>go on a hike</u>.
我想要去健行。

He wants to go home.
他想要回家。

I want to visit China.
我想要去中國大陸。

◆◆◆ 替換看看 ◆◆◆

travel 旅行	travel all over the world 環遊世界
meet different people 認識各式各樣的人	take a group tour 跟團
learn about your country 瞭解你們的國家	try a different style 嘗試不同的風格

2 I'm going to <u>Los Angeles</u> .

我要去洛杉磯。

I'm going to fix the bicycle.

我要修理這輛腳踏車。

I'm going to rent a convertible.

我要租一部敞篷車。

 換個單字意思就不一樣囉

Europe 歐洲	New York 紐約
go camping 露營	bed 上床（睡覺）
play soccer 踢足球	leave 離開

怎樣都要知道的句子

1. 可以這樣說 1-50

- Have you seen the Grand Canyon?
  你參觀過大峽谷嗎？

- Have you been to Italy?
  你去過義大利嗎？

- Where did you go last summer?
  你去年夏天去哪裡？

- We went to Paris.
  我們去巴黎。

- I was there on vacation.
  我在那裡度假。

2. 也可以這樣說

- It's nice to visit old temples.
  去參觀古老的寺廟很不錯。

- It's the best time to see the snow.
  這是賞雪的最佳時機了。

- You shouldn't miss it.
  你絕對不能錯過。

- You should take a bus tour.
  你最好搭公車遊覽。

- Have a nice trip!
  祝旅途愉快！

A：Have you been to America?

B：No, not yet.

A：Are you planning to visit America?

B：Yes, I may visit my sister this summer.

A：That would be great.

A：你去過美國嗎？

B：還沒有。

A：你有計畫去美國旅遊嗎？

B：有啊！我準備這個夏天去找我姊姊。

A：那一定會很棒的！

Unit 8 ★ 運動

你一定會用的句型  1-52

1 I love playing <u>basketball</u>.
我喜歡打籃球。

I love shopping.
我很喜歡購物。

I love cooking.
我很喜歡烹飪。

 替換看看

soccer 足球	golf 高爾夫球
tennis 網球	volleyball 排球
softball 壘球	dodge ball 躲避球

2

I am into <u>soccer</u>.

我很迷足球。

I enjoy playing football.

我很喜歡玩美式足球。

I find tennis very interesting.

我發現網球很有趣。

 換個單字意思就不一樣囉

fishing **釣魚**	surfing **滑水**
yoga **做瑜珈**	rock climbing **攀岩**
skiing **滑雪**	bowling **保齡球**

怎樣都要知道的句子

1. 可以這樣說  1-53

■ What kind of sports do you like?
你喜歡什麼樣的運動？

■ I like swimming.
我喜歡游泳。

■ Do you play golf?
你打高爾夫球嗎？

■ How often do you play?
你多久打一次？

■ I take a jog twice a week.
我一個星期慢跑兩次。

2. 也可以這樣說

■ Let's go watch a game tonight.
我們今晚去看比賽吧！

■ They won by only 1 point.
他們只贏一分。

■ I'm good at sports.
我很擅長運動。

■ I am a sporty girl.
我是個愛運動的女孩。

■ I'm not good at any sports.
我什麼運動都不好。

超常用對話

A：What sports are popular in Taiwan?

B：Well, basketball and baseball are

very popular.

A：Which do you like better, baseball

or basketball?

B：I like basketball better.

A：Are you good at basketball?

B：No. I like watching it on TV.

A：台灣流行什麼運動啊？

B：這個嘛，籃球和棒球很受歡
　　迎。

A：棒球和籃球，你比較喜歡哪
　　一個？

B：我比較喜歡籃球。

A：你很會打籃球嗎？

B：不，我是喜歡看電視上的籃
　　球賽。

Unit 9 ★ 寵物

你一定會用的句型 ⊙ CD 1-55

1 I have a <u>cat</u>.
我有一隻<u>貓</u>。

I have a camera.
我有一台相機。

I have a pencil.
我有一支鉛筆。

◆◆◆ 替換看看 ◆◆◆

dog 狗	rabbit 兔子
snake 蛇	goldfish 金魚
turtle 烏龜	puppy 小狗

2

My pet <u>always obeys me</u>.
我的寵物都很聽我的話。

My pets are wonderful.
我的寵物很棒。

My pet dog is my best friend.
我的寵物狗是我最好的朋友。

 換個單字意思就不一樣囉

bites everything
什麼東西都咬

likes to sleep on my arm
喜歡睡在我手臂上

is a pure-breed
是純種的

is a cross-breed
是配種的

likes to be with people
喜歡和人相處

can shake hands
會握手

怎樣都要知道的句子

1. 可以這樣說 1-56

- Do you have any pets?
  你有養寵物嗎？

- I have never seen such a lovely pet.
  我從沒看過這麼可愛的寵物。

- What's its name?
  牠叫什麼名字？

- What kind of food does it eat?
  牠吃什麼樣的食物？

- Come here!
  過來這裡！

2. 也可以這樣說

- I found her on the street.
  我在街上找到她的。

- He barks at strangers.
  他會對陌生人叫。

- I take it for a walk every day.
  我每天都會帶牠去散個步。

- She is part of the family.
  她是這家庭的一份子。

- I took him to a vet.
  我帶他去看了獸醫。

1-57

A：Do you have a pet?

B：No, we don't. My husband
doesn't like animals.

A：Really?

B：Yeah. But I like animals.

A：That's a shame. My wife loves
dogs, so we have two dogs. She
runs with them every morning.

A：你們有養寵物嗎？

B：沒有。我老公不喜歡動
物。

A：真的嗎？

B：是啊，但我喜歡動物。

A：那太可惜了。我老婆很喜
歡狗，所以我們有養兩隻
狗。她每天早上都帶著牠
們一起去跑步。

Unit 10 ★ 算命

你一定會用的句型　CD 1-58

1

I'm a/an <u>Gemini</u>.
我是<u>雙子座</u>。

He is a Virgo.
他是處女座的。

My father is an Aquarius.
我爸爸是水瓶座的。

 替換看看

Aries 白羊座	Taurus 金牛座
Cancer 巨蟹座	Leo 獅子座
Virgo 處女座	Libra 天秤座

2

Pisces are very artistic.
雙魚座非常有藝術氣息。

You are very kind.
你很和善。

Our kids are very intelligent.
我們的小孩非常聰明。

 換個單字意思就不一樣囉

Scorpios／elegant
天蠍座／高雅

Sagittariuses／active
射手座／活潑

Capricorns／stubborn
摩羯座／倔強

Aquariuses／responsible
水瓶座／負責任

Leos／optimistic
獅子座／樂觀

Virgos／picky
處女座／吹毛求疵

怎樣都要知道的句子

1. 可以這樣說  1-59

- What's your Zodiac sign?
  你是什麼星座的呢？

- Do you believe in fortune-telling?
  你相信算命嗎？

- I can read palms a little.
  我略通手相。

- You can try red wooden blocks at the temple.
  你可以去寺廟試試看擲筊。

- 'Daan' is a lucky day.
  「大安」表示幸運日。

2. 也可以這樣說

- I am really out of luck!
  我的運氣真差！

- Was that bad luck?
  那個（的意思）是壞運氣嗎？

- A big nose will bring you a fortune.
  大鼻子會為你帶來財富。

- Palm reading is very popular.
  看手相很流行。

- I'm interested in the Zodiac.
  我對星座很感興趣。

1-60

A：Do you believe in fortune-telling?

B：No, I don't. But I'm interested in
the Zodiac.

A：You're a Virgo, right?

B：Yeah, and Virgos are very hard-
working.

A：Don't forget about the picky part.

A：你相信算命嗎？

B：不，我不相信。不過我對星
座很有興趣。

A：你是處女座的，對吧？

B：是啊，而處女座的人都很認
真努力。

A：別忘了還有挑剔啊。

Unit 11 ★ 風俗習慣

你一定會用的句型　CD 1-61

1

What do/did you do for <u>Lantern Festival</u>?
你們<u>元宵節</u>那天都做些什麼呢？

What do you do on Sundays?
你星期天都做什麼呢？

What do you do on your days off?
你放假時都做什麼呢？

◆◆◆ 替換看看 ◆◆◆

Valentine's Day 情人節	Mother's Day 母親節
Christmas 聖誕節	Dragon Boat Festival 端午節
Moon Festival 中秋節	your 30th anniversary 你們的三十周年慶

2

Your <u>forests</u> are beautiful.
你們的<u>森林</u>很漂亮。

The scenery was amazing.
景色實在太美了。

The museums are wonderful.
博物館很棒。

 換個單字意思就不一樣囉

mountains
山

buildings
建築物

temples
寺廟

gardens
庭院

women
女性

lakes
湖泊

怎樣都要知道的句子

- I like rice and noodles.
  我喜歡飯還有麵。

- Soy milk is really good.
  豆漿很好喝。

- Tai-chi is very good for your health.
  太極對你的健康非常有益。

- Kids receive red envelopes from adults on New Year's Eve.　小孩子在除夕夜那天會收到大人給的紅包。

- We don't dress in black when we go to a wedding.　我們不會穿著黑衣服去參加婚禮。

2. 也可以這樣說

- I stay with my family on New Year's Eve.
  除夕夜那天，我和我的家人聚在一起。

- When is Dragon-boat Festival?
  端午節是什麼時候？

- What do you do for Lantern Festival?
  元宵節時你們都會做什麼呢？

- Chinese holidays are based on the lunar calendar.　中國的節日是依據陰曆而定。

- Today is Chinese Valentine's Day.
  今天是中國情人節（七夕）。

CD 1-63

A：How do you like Taiwan,
　　Robert?

B：I love Taiwan! Your food is
　　great, and your people are kind.

A：I'm glad to hear that!

B：Oh, and I enjoyed celebrating
　　the Moon Festival with you.

A：Great!

A：你還喜歡台灣嗎，羅伯
　　特？

B：我愛台灣！你們的食物很
　　好吃，而且人民又親切。

A：我很高興聽你這麼說！

B：噢，而且我和你們一起慶
　　祝中秋節很開心。

A：很好！

Note

Chapter 3 拜訪老外

Unit 1 ★ 打電話

你一定會用的句型 1-64

1 May I <u>speak to Smith</u>?
我可以和史密斯說話嗎？

May I close the window?
我可以把窗戶關上嗎？

May I come in?
我可以進來嗎？

◆◆◆ 替換看看 ◆◆◆

speak to a sales person 和業務員說話	talk to your manager 和你的經理說話
talk to your section chief 和你們部門的負責人說話	ask where he went 問他去了哪裡
leave a message 留個口信	have your name 知道您的名字

2 Please tell him <u>to call me at home</u>.

請叫（告訴）他<u>打我家裡的電話</u>。

Please tell him to call Bill.

請叫他打給比爾。

Please tell her I said hello.

請幫我向她問好。

◆◆◆ 換個單字意思就不一樣囉 ◆◆◆

to call my cell phone 打我的手機	that I called 我有打來
that I will call again 我會再打過來	that I will be late 我會遲到
to call me back 回我電話	that Jessica wants to speak to him 潔西卡想跟他談談

怎樣都要知道的句子

1. 可以這樣説

■ Hello!
喂！

■ May I speak to Sandra, please?
我可以和珊卓拉說話嗎？

■ This is Helen speaking.
我是海倫。

■ Can you talk now?
你現在方便說話嗎？

■ Sorry to call you at dinner time.
很抱歉在晚餐的時間打電話給你。

2. 也可以這樣説

■ When will he be back?
他什麼時候會回來？

■ May I leave a message?
我可以留個口信嗎？

■ I see. I'll call again.
我知道了。我會再打電話過來的。

■ Please tell him that I called.
請轉告他說我有打來。

■ My phone number is 02-1234-5678.
我的電話是02-1234-5678。

1-66

A：Hello.

B：Hello. This is Mary speaking.

　　May I talk to George, please?

A：I'm sorry. He's out now.

B：Would you tell him that I

　　called?

A：Sure, I will.

B：Thank you. Good-bye.

A：喂。

B：喂，我是瑪麗，我可以和喬治說話嗎？

A：不好意思，他現在不在家喔。

B：你可以轉告他說我有打電話來嗎？

A：當然，我會的。

B：謝謝你，再見。

Unit 2 ★ 接電話

你一定會用的句型 CD 1-67

1 She's <u>out right now</u>.
她現在不在。

She's in the middle of a meeting.
她正在開會。

She's not home at this moment.
她現在不在家。

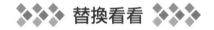
替換看看

not here 不在這裡	in the bath now 正在洗澡
out with her friends 和她的朋友出去了	on another line 正在通電話
away from her desk 不在位子上	not available 無法接聽電話

2 She should be back <u>soon</u>.

她應該很快就會回來了。

I should be back by then.

我那時候應該就回來了。

They should be here by noon.

他們應該中午就到這裡了。

 換個單字意思就不一樣囉

in a little while	in a couple of hours
再過一會兒	再過幾個小時
by three	by dinner
三點以前	晚餐以前
real soon	before ten o'clock
很快	十點以前

怎樣都要知道的句子

1. 可以這樣說  1-68

- Who is calling?
  你是哪位？

- Would you speak more slowly?
  你可以說慢一點嗎？

- She went to work today.
  她今天去上班了。

- I don't know what time she'll be back.
  我不曉得她幾點會回來。

- Shall I have him call you back?
  我請他回電給你好嗎？

2. 也可以這樣說

- May I take a message?
  我替你留個口信好嗎？

- I'll tell him that you called.
  我會轉告他說你有打電話過來的。

- Does he know your number?
  他知道你的電話號碼嗎？

- One moment, please.
  請稍等一下。

- Please hold.
  請稍等一下。

CD 1-69

A：Lisa Parker's office.

B：Hi, this is James, Lisa's husband.

Can I speak to her, please?

A：I'm sorry, Mr. Parker. Lisa is out

now. Would you like to leave a

message?

B：Well…when is she coming back?

A：She should be back in two hours.

A：莉莎派克辦公室。

B：嗨，我是莉莎的先生詹姆斯。我可以跟她說個話嗎？

A：很抱歉，派克先生，莉莎現在不在。您要留言給她嗎？

B：嗯…她什麼時候會回來？

A：她應該在兩小時之內會回來。

Unit 3 ★ 打錯電話

你一定會用的句型  1-70

1

<u>I am sorry</u> , I called the wrong number.
<u>我很抱歉</u>，我撥錯電話了。

I'm sorry, who's calling?
不好意思，你是哪位？

I'm sorry to hear the news.
聽到這消息，我深感遺憾。

◆◆◆ 替換看看 ◆◆◆

Sorry 抱歉	I apologize 我道歉
I guess 我猜想	Excuse me 不好意思
I think I made a mistake 我想我弄錯了	I'm terribly sorry 我真的非常抱歉

2

Is this <u>25-8844</u>?

這裡是25-8844嗎？

Is this for sale?

這些是在拍賣的嗎？

Is this for women?

這是給女性的嗎？

 換個單字意思就不一樣囉

Miss Glen's house 格蘭小姐家	Mrs. Kent's office 肯特太太的辦公室
an English school 一間英語學校	the sales department 銷售部
Carter's Grocery Store 卡特雜貨店	the principal's office 校長辦公室

怎樣都要知道的句子

1. 可以這樣說 1-71

- Sorry, you have the wrong number.
  抱歉，你打錯電話了。

- What number did you call?
  你撥幾號呢？

- There's no Terry here.
  這裡沒有泰瑞這個人。

- You should check the number again.
  你應該再檢查一次電話號碼。

- Who are you calling?
  你要找誰？

2. 也可以這樣說

- Sorry, I called the wrong number.
  抱歉，我打錯電話了。

- Is this 02-1234-4678?
  這裡是02–1234–4678嗎？

- Is this an English school?
  這裡是間英語學校嗎？

- I'm sorry.
  我很抱歉。

- That's okay.
  沒關係。

1-72

A：Hello?

B：Hello. This is Mary. Can I speak to George?

A：I'm afraid you have the wrong number.

B：Is this 25-8844?

A：No, it isn't.

B：Oh, I'm sorry. Thank you.

A：喂？

B：喂，我是瑪麗，可以請喬治聽電話嗎？

A：我想你打錯電話了。

B：這裡是25-8844嗎？

A：不，並不是。

B：噢，我很抱歉。謝謝你。

Unit 4 ★ 約時間

你一定會用的句型  1-73

1

Do you have time next <u>Friday</u>?
下個禮拜五你有空嗎？

Do you have a vacant room?
你有空房間嗎？

Do you have road maps?
你有道路地圖嗎？

 替換看看

Sunday 星期天	Monday 星期一	Tuesday 星期二
Wednesday 星期三	Thursday 星期四	Friday 星期五
Saturday 星期六		

2

I'll be there by seven o'clock.
我七點之前會到那裡。

I'll be there before 9:00 p.m.
我九點之前會到那裡。

I'll be here for another hour.
我還會在這裡待一個小時。

 換個單字意思就不一樣囉

three o'clock
三點鐘

four o'clock
四點鐘

six o'clock
六點鐘

seven o'clock
七點鐘

eight o'clock
八點鐘

eleven o'clock
十一點鐘

109

怎樣都要知道的句子

1. 可以這樣說 1-74

■ Are you free next Monday?
下禮拜一你有空嗎？

■ Let's go out for dinner.
我們出去吃個晚餐吧。

■ My parents want to meet you.
我的父母想要見見你。

■ Sure. I'd love to.
當然，我很願意。

■ Sorry. I'll be busy next week.
抱歉，我下禮拜很忙。

2. 也可以這樣說

■ When shall we meet?
我們什麼時候見面呢？

■ How about tomorrow night?
明天晚上如何？

■ It's up to you.
看你囉。（你決定囉）

■ I'll check my schedule.
我會看一下我的行程。

■ Let's meet at the station.
我們在車站碰面吧。

CD 1-75

A：Do you have time next Friday?

B：I'm free then. What's up?

A：We are having a party. Do you want to come?

B：I'd love to. Should I bring anything?

A：Nope. We'll take care of it.

A：下個禮拜五，你有空嗎？

B：我那時候有空。什麼事？

A：我們要辦一個派對，你要來嗎？

B：我很樂意。我應該帶些什麼東西嗎？

A：不用，我們會打理好一切的。

Unit 5 ★ 帶到家裡

你一定會用的句型 CD 1-76

1 Why don't you <u>get a cab</u>?
你為什麼不叫輛計程車呢？

Why don't you come with us?
你為什麼不和我們一起去呢？

Why don't you try on this shirt?
你何不試穿看看這件襯衫呢？

◆◆◆ 替換看看 ◆◆◆

come in 進來	call me to pick you up 打電話叫我去接你
stay for dinner 留下來吃晚餐	join us 加入我們
call her 打電話給她	go home 回家

2

If you <u>get lost</u>, please call me.

如果你迷路了，請打電話給我。

If you didn't do that, please tell me.

如果那不是你做的，請你告訴我。

If you don't take that job, please let me know.

如果你不要接受那份工作，請跟我說一聲。

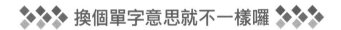 換個單字意思就不一樣囉

need anything **需要任何東西**	can come **可以來**
have time **有時間**	are in trouble **有麻煩**
want to talk **想要聊天**	forgive me **原諒我**

怎樣都要知道的句子

1. 可以這樣說  1-77

- Take the Worcester Line and get off at the first stop.
  搭渥斯特線，然後在第一個停靠站下車。

- Let's meet at the front door.
  我們在前門碰面吧。

- Please call me when you arrive.
  你到的時候請打電話給我。

- I'll draw you a map.
  我畫張地圖給你。

- If you get lost, please call me.
  如果你迷路的話，請打電話給我。

2. 也可以這樣說

- Please come on in.
  請進。

- Take off your shoes here, please.
  麻煩請在這裡脫鞋子。

- Please have a seat.
  請坐。

- Please make yourself at home.
  請把這裡當自己的家。（隨意）

- This is from my husband.
  這是我丈夫給的（禮物）。

CD 1-78

A：Come on in, Susan! Your room is over there.

B：Thanks, John. I had a hard time finding your house, actually.

A：Why didn't you call me, then?

B：I didn't have my cell phone with me.

A：I see. Well, just tell me if you need anything.

A：請進，蘇珊，妳的房間在那邊。

B：謝謝，約翰。其實我花了好大的功夫才找到你家呢。

A：那妳為什麼沒打電話給我呢？

B：我沒有帶我的手機。

A：我懂了。那麼，如果妳需要什麼就跟我說吧。

Unit 6 ★ 進入老外的家

你一定會用的句型 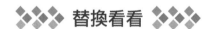 CD 1-79

1

Nice <u>house</u>!

好棒的房子！

Nice day!

好棒的一天！

Nice shirt!

好棒的襯衫！

◆◆◆ 替換看看 ◆◆◆

car 車	curtains 窗簾
living room 客廳	garden 院子
bedroom 臥房	dress 洋裝

2 You have a/an <u>beautiful home</u>.
你有一間很漂亮的家。

We have two tickets.
我們有兩張票。

She has a camera.
她有一台相機。

 換個單字意思就不一樣囉

lovely daughter
很可愛的女兒

big house
很大的房子

cute dog
很可愛的狗

wonderful garden
很棒的院子

amazing cook
很厲害的廚師

really nice sofa
很棒的沙發

怎樣都要知道的句子

1. 可以這樣說  1-80

- Good evening!
  晚安！

- Thank you for inviting me.
  謝謝你邀請我。

- I'm sorry that I'm a little late(early).
  抱歉我來晚（早）了一點。

- You live in a nice place.
  你家真是不錯。

- Should I put my shoes outside?
  我是不是應該把鞋子放在外面呢？

- This is a small present.
  這是個小禮物。

2. 也可以這樣說

- Hello! Please come in.
  哈囉！請進。

- Please hang your overcoat here.
  請把你的大衣掛在這裡。

- I'm glad you like it.
  我很高興你喜歡。

- The other guests are in the library.
  其他的客人都在圖書館裡。

- Make yourself at home.
  把這裡當自己家吧。

CD 1-81

A：Welcome, Mary. Come on in.

B：Thank you for your invitation.

A：The pleasure is ours. Have a seat, please.

B：Thank you.

A：This is our living room.

B：Wow! Nice house! The table looks beautiful.

A：歡迎啊，瑪麗。請進。

B：謝謝你的邀請。

A：那是我們的榮幸。請坐。

B：謝謝你。

A：這裡是我們的客廳。

B：哇！好棒的房子！桌子好漂亮。

你一定會用的句型 2-1

1

I have <u>two daughters</u>.

我有兩個女兒。

I have two dogs.

我有（養）兩隻狗。

I have no money.

我沒有錢。

◆◆◆ 替換看看 ◆◆◆

a beautiful wife 一個美麗的妻子	three kids 三個小孩
a pet cat 一隻寵物貓	two cousins 兩個姪子（外甥）
a lot of friends 很多朋友	only one son 一個獨生子

2

Jeff, this is Ana. Ana, this is Jeff.
傑夫，這位是安娜。安娜，這位是傑夫。

This is Jenny.
這位是珍妮。

Ken, this is Mr. Brown.Mr. Brown, this is Ken.
肯，這位是布朗先生。布朗先生，這位是肯。

◆◆◆ 換個單字意思就不一樣囉 ◆◆◆

Kate ／Susan ／
Susan ／Kate
凱特／蘇珊／蘇珊／凱特

Ben ／my dad ／
Dad ／Ben
班／我爸爸／爸爸／班

Joe／Mr. Carson ／
Mr. Carson ／Joe
喬／卡森先生／卡森先生／喬

Lisa／my mom／
Mom ／my friend, Lisa
麗莎／我媽媽／媽媽／我的朋友麗莎

George ／Emma／
Emma ／George
喬治／艾瑪／艾瑪／喬治

Frank ／Mrs. Hsieh ／
Mrs. Hsieh ／Frank
法蘭克／謝太太／謝太太／法蘭克

怎樣都要知道的句子

1. 可以這樣說　 2-2

- Let me introduce my family.
  讓我來介紹一下我的家人。

- This is Edward. He is my brother.
  這位是艾德華。他是我弟弟（哥哥）。

- I have two sons and a daughter.
  我有兩個兒子、一個女兒。

- My father isn't home today.
  我爸爸今天不在家。

- My husband works for Google.
  我丈夫在Google工作。

2. 也可以這樣說

- Both my parents work.
  我的父母都在工作。

- Our son is studying abroad.
  我們的兒子在海外唸書。

- My brother is three years older than me.
  我哥哥比我大三歲。

- We look alike.
  我們長得很像。

- We are the opposite.
  我們完全南轅北轍。

CD 2-3.

A：This is a picture of my family.

B：Who is this little boy?

A：He is my nephew. He is three

　　years old.

B：He is lovely. What is his

　　name?

A：His name is Tom.

A：這是一張我家人的照片。

B：這個小男孩是誰？

A：他是我的姪子，他三歲大。

B：他真是可愛，他叫什麼名字

　　啊？

A：他的名字叫湯姆。

Unit 8 ★ 一起進餐

你一定會用的句型　CD 2-4

1

It is <u>delicious</u>.
這<u>真好吃</u>。

It is wonderful.
這太神奇了。

It is almost ready.
差不多可以用餐了。

◆◆◆ 替換看看 ◆◆◆

too sweet 太甜了	crispy 真酥脆
expensive 太貴了	hot 好燙
good 太棒了	broken 壞了

2 Would you please pass me the <u>pepper</u>?
可以麻煩你拿胡椒粉給我嗎？

Would you please sit down?
請你坐下。

Would you please pass the rolls around?
可以請你把小麵包傳給大家嗎？

◆◆◆ 換個單字意思就不一樣囉 ◆◆◆

salt 鹽巴	butter 奶油
bread 麵包	salad 沙拉
milk 牛奶	dish 盤子

怎樣都要知道的句子

1. 可以這樣說 2-5.

- It's time to eat.
  該吃飯了。

- It smells good!
  好香喔！

- Would you please pass me the salt?
  請幫我拿一下鹽巴。

- Here you are!
  給你。

- Would you like some more?
  你還要再來一些嗎？

2. 也可以這樣說

- I hope you'd like Taiwanese food.
  我希望你會喜歡台灣料理。

- That's my favorite.
  那是我最愛吃的。

- You cook very well.
  你真會煮菜。

- Would you give me the recipe?
  可以給我食譜嗎？

- I'm so full.
  我吃得好飽。

CD 2-6

A：Dinner is ready!

B：What are we having for dinner?

A：Steak!

B：Wow! It looks delicious.

A：I hope you will like it.

B：Don't worry. Steak is my favorite.

A：晚餐好囉！

B：我們今天晚餐吃什麼呢？

A：吃牛排。

B：哇！看起來真好吃。

A：我希望你會喜歡這料理。

B：別擔心，牛排是我的最愛。

你一定會用的句型　 2-7

1

May I <u>join you</u>?
我可以加入你們嗎？

May I have another beer?
我可以再要一瓶啤酒嗎？

May I put my seat back?
我可以把椅子往後靠嗎？

◆◆◆ 替換看看 ◆◆◆

get in 進來	see that 看看那個
try it 試試看	sit here 坐這裡
buy you a drink 請你喝杯飲料	talk to you 跟你說話

2 Nice party, isn't it?

很棒的一場派對，對吧？

It's interesting, isn't it?

那真是有趣，對吧？

That's a good idea, isn't it?

那真是個好主意，對吧？

◆◆◆ 換個單字意思就不一樣囉 ◆◆◆

Great party
很棒的派對

Nice song
很棒的歌

Excellent food
很棒的食物

A wonderful night
一個美好的夜晚

Good idea
好主意

Great show
很棒的表演

怎樣都要知道的句子

1. 可以這樣説 2-8

- Please introduce me to your friends.
  請把我介紹給你的朋友們。

- I'm so pleased to meet you.
  我非常高興認識你。

- Please call me Ken.
  請叫我肯。

- I'm Debra. You can just call me Deb.
  我是黛博拉。你可以叫我小黛。

- I've heard a lot about you.
  我聽說了很多你的事蹟。

2. 也可以這樣説

- May I join you?
  我可以加入你們嗎？

- Is this seat taken?
  這裡有人坐嗎？

- Can I buy you a drink?
  我可以請你喝杯飲料嗎？

- Do you have a light?
  你有打火機嗎？

- Let's play pool.
  我們來打撞球吧。

CD 2-9

A：There are many people here.

B：Nice party, isn't it?

A：Yes, it is. By the way, do you know that girl?

B：Yes. She's my friend, Mary.

A：Will you introduce me to her?

B：Sure, no problem.

A：這裡人真多。

B：很棒的派對，不是嗎？

A：是啊。對了，你認識那個女生嗎？

B：認識啊，她是我朋友瑪麗。

A：可以把我介紹給她認識嗎？

B：當然，沒問題。

Unit **10** ★ 聊天技巧

1

I like <u>your hair</u>.
我喜歡你的頭髮。

I like skiing and tennis.
我喜歡滑雪和網球。

I like it very much.
我好喜歡這個。

◆◆◆ 替換看看 ◆◆◆

your dress 你的洋裝	sports 運動
classical music 古典樂	talking to you 和你聊天
your magic tricks 你的魔術	this coat 這件外套

132

2 How's <u>your family</u>?
你的家人還好嗎？

How's Mary?
瑪麗還好嗎？

How's everything?
一切都還好嗎？

 換個單字意思就不一樣囉

your mother 你母親	your job 你的工作
your steak 你的牛排	the food 食物
work 工作	your weekend 你的週末

怎樣都要知道的句子

1. 可以這樣説 2-11

- What do you do?
  你是做什麼的？

- I'd like to hear about it.
  我想聽聽相關的事情。

- I'm interested.
  我很有興趣。

- How did it go?
  進行得如何？

- That's great.
  那太好了。

2. 也可以這樣説

- Would you like to dance?
  你想要跳舞嗎？

- That's a pretty dress.
  那洋裝真漂亮。

- What's your sign?
  你是什麼星座的？

- Don't I know you from somewhere?
  我是不是在哪個地方見過你啊？

- Do you mind if I smoke?
  你介意我抽菸嗎？

超常用對話

2-12

A：What do you do, Tom?

B：I study in law school.

A：So, are you going to be a lawyer?

B：Yes, of course.

A：That's wonderful.

B：What about you? What do you do?

A：I'm a writer.

A：你是做什麼的，湯姆？

B：我在法學院唸書。

A：那麼你以後要當個律師囉？

B：是啊，當然。

A：那很棒啊。

B：那麼你呢？你是做什麼的？

A：我是個作家。

你一定會用的句型

 2-13

1

It's time to <u>go home</u>.
該是回家的時候了。

It's time to go to school.
該是上學的時候了。

It's time to tell you the truth.
該是告訴你真相的時候了。

◆◆◆ 替換看看 ◆◆◆

clean up 清理	go out 出門
say good-bye 說再見	leave 離開
go to bed 上床睡覺	go 走

2

<u>Everything</u> was so nice.
一切都很棒。

He was so kind.
他人真是和善。

It was so cold.
天氣好冷。

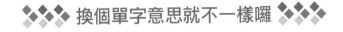 換個單字意思就不一樣囉

The food
食物

Everyone
大家

The music
音樂

The cocktail
雞尾酒

The host
主持人

The cake
蛋糕

怎樣都要知道的句子

1. 可以這樣說  2-14

- I think I have to go now.
  我想我現在該走了。

- I really enjoyed the party.
  我真的在派對玩得很開心。

- Everything was so nice.
  一切都很棒。

- Dinner was just delicious.
  晚餐真是太好吃了。

- It's been nice talking with you.
  跟你聊天很愉快。

2. 也可以這樣說

- How about getting you a car?
  幫你叫個車怎麼樣？

- Could I give you a lift?
  我能載你一程嗎？

- We'll see you again.
  我們回頭見。

- Thanks for coming.
  謝謝你來。

- Please come to our house next time.
  下次請來我家玩。

2-15

A：It was a great party, Mr. and Mrs. Rose.

B：Thank you, Amy. I hope you enjoyed it.

A：Yes, I did. And meeting new people was fun.

B：Good! Thanks for coming, Amy!

A：Thank you for inviting me.

A：派對很棒，羅斯先生、羅斯太太。

B：謝謝妳，艾咪，我希望妳玩得很開心。

A：有啊，而且認識新朋友很有趣。

B：那就好！謝謝妳來，艾咪！

A：謝謝你們邀請我。

Note

Chapter 4 輕鬆生活‧旅遊

你一定會用的句型 CD 2-16

1

Is it near the <u>train station</u>?

它離火車站近嗎？

Is it far from here?

它離這裡很遠嗎？

Is it on this street?

它是在這條街上嗎？

◆◆◆ 替換看看 ◆◆◆

post office 郵局	shopping mall 購物中心
park 公園	bank 銀行
stationary store 文具店	drugstore 藥局

2 You have to pay <u>the gas</u>.
你必須付<u>瓦斯費</u>。

We have to send a letter.
我們必須去寄信。

You have to leave now.
你必須現在離開。

 換個單字意思就不一樣囉

the heat
暖氣費

the electricity
電費

your own
electricity
你自己的電費

extra money
額外的錢

a deposit
一筆訂金

seven thousand
dollars a month
一個月七千元

143

怎樣都要知道的句子

1. 可以這樣說  2-17

- I'm looking for a one-bedroom apartment.
  我在找一間單房的公寓。

- How much is the rent?
  房租多少錢？

- Is there an elevator?
  有電梯嗎？

- Are utilities included?
  有包含公用設備（水電、煤氣）嗎？

- I'd like a view of the lake.
  我希望可以看到湖。

2. 也可以這樣說

- I am looking for a part-time job.
  我在找一份兼職的工作。

- Are you hiring?
  你們有在徵人嗎？

- What is the salary?
  薪水怎麼算？

- I have a master's degree.
  我有碩士學位。

- Any work experience?
  有工作經驗嗎？

CD 2-18

A: May I help you?

B: Yes, I'm looking for a one-
bedroom apartment.

A: What's your budget?

B: Well, five hundred a moth.

A：我可以幫您嗎？

B：是的，麻煩你。我在找一
間單房的公寓。

A：您的預算是多少呢？

B：這個嘛，一個月五千元。

Unit 2 ★ 超市

你一定會用的句型

 2-19

1 What aisle is the <u>sugar</u> in?
糖放在哪一個走道上呢？

What time is she arriving?
她幾點會到呢？

What book are you looking for?
你在找哪一本書呢？

◆◆◆ 替換看看 ◆◆◆

shampoo 洗髮精	flour 麵粉
canned food 罐頭	milk 牛奶
cereal 穀片	salt 鹽

2 Do you have any <u>dish soap</u>?
你們有<u>洗碗精嗎</u>？

Do you have the directions?
你知道路嗎？

Do you have to leave now?
你們一定要現在離開嗎？

 換個單字意思就不一樣囉

cabbage 高麗菜	eggs 蛋
coffee 咖啡	ketchup 番茄醬
chocolate 巧克力	bananas 香蕉

怎樣都要知道的句子

 2-20

1. 可以這樣說

■ Excuse me. Where are the onions?
不好意思，請問洋蔥放在哪裡？

■ It's at the back.
它在後面。

■ I'll ask a shop clerk for you.
我幫你問一下店員。

■ Do I line up here?
是在這裡排隊嗎？

■ Are you the last in line?
你是排隊的最後一個嗎？

2. 也可以這樣說

■ I can't find the chocolate.
我找不到巧克力（在哪裡）。

■ Do you have any dish soap?
你們有洗碗精嗎？

■ Can I have an extra bag?
可以再多給我一個袋子嗎？

■ I don't need a plastic bag, thank you.
我不需要塑膠袋，謝謝你。

■ Can I use a credit card?
我可以刷信用卡嗎？

CD 2-21

A：Excuse me. Do you have paper cups?

B：Yes, of course. They're behind the baby products.

A：And where are the baby products?

B：Right there, ma'am.

A：Oh, I see it. Thank you.

A：不好意思，你們有（賣）紙杯嗎？

B：當然有。它們在嬰兒用品的後面。

A：那麼嬰兒用品在哪裡呢？

B：就在那裡，小姐。

A：噢，我看到了，謝謝你。

Unit **3** ★ 百貨公司

你一定會用的句型  2-22

1

Is there a <u>department store</u> in this area?
這一帶有<u>百貨公司</u>嗎？

Is there a school near here?
這附近有學校嗎？

Is there a card on the table?
桌上有一張卡片嗎？

◆◆◆ 替換看看 ◆◆◆

shopping mall 購物商場	grocery store 雜貨店
supermarket 超級市場	convenience store 便利商店
sporting goods store 運動用品店	book store 書局

2 Where is/are <u>women's wear</u>?
女裝在哪裡？

Where is the entrance?
入口在哪裡？

Where is the fitting room?
試衣間在哪裡？

 換個單字意思就不一樣囉

men's wear
男裝

children's wear
童裝

home appliances
家電

the pharmacy
藥品

the information desk
服務台

the entrance ／ exit
入口／出口

怎樣都要知道的句子

1. 可以這樣說  2-23

■ May I help you?
我可以幫您嗎？

■ Where is the toy department?
玩具部在哪裡？

■ I'm looking for men's shoes.
我在找男用鞋。

■ It's on the third floor.
它在三樓。

■ Take the elevator.
請坐電梯。

2. 也可以這樣說

■ That's a real bargain.
那真是太划算了。

■ Is this for men or women?
這是給男生的還是女生的？

■ Can I see this?
我可看看這個嗎？

■ I'm just looking.
我只是看看。

■ Can you wrap it for me?
你可以幫我包裝一下嗎？

超常用對話

CD 2-24

A：May I help you?

B：Yes. I'm looking for a T-shirt.

A：How about these?

B：Hmm… Do you have larger

ones?

A：Yes, we do. Here they are.

B：Let's see… I like this one.

May I try it on?

A：我可以為您效勞嗎？

B：是的，我在找襯衫。

A：這些怎麼樣？

B：嗯…你們有沒有比較大的

襯衫？

A：有的。就是這些。

B：我看看…我喜歡這件。我

可以試穿嗎？

Unit 4 ★ 銀行

1

I'd like to <u>cash a check</u>.
我想要兌現一張支票。

I'd like to stay here.
我想要待在這裡。

I'd like to order 3 cups of coffee.
我要點三杯咖啡。

◆◆◆ 替換看看 ◆◆◆

make a deposit 存錢	transfer money 轉帳
make a transfer 轉帳	open an account 開戶
close my account 解約帳戶	apply for a loan 申請貸款

2 How many <u>pounds</u> to the dollar?
美元兌換英鎊的匯率是多少？

How many days did you stay?
你待了幾天？

How many times have you been there?
你去過那裡多少次了？

 換個單字意思就不一樣囉

Francs 法郎	Yen 日圓
New Taiwan Dollars 新台幣	Rupees 盧比
Pesos 披索	Euros 歐元

怎樣都要知道的句子

1. 可以這樣說 2-26

- Is there a bank near here?
  這附近有銀行嗎？

- Would you cash these traveler's checks?
  你可以兌現這些旅遊支票嗎？

- With some change, please.
  請給我一些零錢。

- Into ten dollar bills, please.
  麻煩請都換成十塊錢。

- May I see your ID?
  我可以看一下您的身分證嗎？

2. 也可以這樣說

- I'd like to open a savings account.
  我想要開立一個存款帳戶。

- What' the interest rate?
  利率是多少？

- Are you a customer here?
  您是這裡的顧客嗎？

- Press your PIN number here.
  請在此鍵入您的個人識別號碼。

- You need to fill in that form first.
  您得先把那張表格填妥。

2-27

A：Good afternoon, sir. How may I help you?

B：I'd like to cash a check, please.

A：No problem.

B：And I'd also like to make a deposit.

A：Sure. Please fill out this form first.

A：午安，先生，我該如何為您效勞呢？

B：麻煩你，我想要兌現一張支票。

A：沒問題。

B：我還想要存錢。

A：當然。請先填好這個表格。

Unit 5 ★ 郵局

你 一 定 會 用 的 句 型  2-28

1

I need <u>some stamps</u>, please.
我需要一些郵票，謝謝。

I need another vacation.
我還需要放一次假。

I need a haircut.
我需要剪個頭髮。

 替換看看

an envelope 一個信封	to send a letter 寄一封信
to send a parcel 寄一件包裹	a mail-order catalogue 一份郵購產品目錄
the Zip code 郵遞區號	your return address 寄件人地址

2 By <u>air mail</u> to Taiwan, please.
寄到台灣的**航空**信,謝謝。

I go to school by bus.
我搭公車上學。

He practices English by speaking with native speakers.
他和母語人士交談來練習英文。

 換個單字意思就不一樣囉

registered mail
掛號件

express mail
特快件

overnight mail
隔夜特快件

surface mail
平信(使用地面運輸工具)

first-class mail
特急件

prompt mail
即時件

怎樣都要知道的句子

1. 可以這樣說  2-29

- Excuse me, I want to mail this.
  不好意思，我想要寄這個。

- How much is the postage?
  郵資是多少錢？

- Air mail, please.
  航空信，謝謝。

- First class, please.
  特急件，謝謝。

- What's inside?
  裡面裝的是什麼？

2. 也可以這樣說

- What is the cheapest way to send this?
  寄這個最便宜的方式是什麼？

- Just put this into the mailbox.
  把這個投入郵筒就可以了。

- Can you weigh this?
  你可以秤一下這個的重量嗎？

- How long will it take?
  那會花上多久時間？

- I need some stamps, please.
  我需要一些郵票，謝謝。

 2-30

A：What can I do for you?

B：I need to send a letter by air mail to Japan.

A：Sure, but I need your return address, please.

B：OK. How much is the postage?

A：26 dollars.

A：我能為您做什麼呢？

B：我要寄一封航空信件到日本。

A：當然，但我需要寄件人地址，麻煩您。

B：好的。郵資多少？

A：二十六塊錢。

Unit 6 ★ 餐廳

你一定會用的句型  2-31

1

Do they have <u>seafood</u>?
他們有海鮮嗎？

Do you have a dress code?
你們有服儀規定嗎？

Do you have green tea?
你們有綠茶嗎？

◆◆◆ 替換看看 ◆◆◆

steak 牛排	beef 牛肉
iced coffee 冰咖啡	broccoli 花椰菜
stew 燉菜	lamb 羊肉

2 How is the <u>wine list</u>?
酒類的清單怎麼樣？

How is the weather?
天氣如何？

How is the steak?
牛排怎麼樣？

❖❖❖ 換個單字意思就不一樣囉 ❖❖❖

soup 湯	cake 蛋糕
asparagus 蘆筍	pan cake 煎餅
sausage 香腸	appetizer 開胃菜

怎樣都要知道的句子

1. 可以這樣說  2-32

- Let's have dinner now.
  我們現在來吃晚餐吧。

- Well, what shall we eat?
  嗯，我們要吃什麼呢？

- What would you like to eat?
  你想要吃什麼呢？

- I know a good Italian restaurant.
  我知道一間很棒的義大利餐廳。

- You should try that restaurant.
  你應該去那間餐廳試試。

2. 也可以這樣說

- The food there is very good.
  那裡的餐點很好吃。

- They also have a variety of cakes.
  他們還有很多種類的蛋糕。

- They use very fresh vegetables.
  他們使用的蔬菜非常新鮮。

- I don't feel like eating pizza now.
  我現在不想吃披薩。

- It's a little expensive, I think.
  我覺得它有點貴。

超常用對話

CD 2-33

A: Would you like to have dinner?

B: Yes, I am hungry.

A: Me too. I know a good Italian restaurant.

B: That's great. Let's go.

A：你想吃晚餐嗎？

B：好啊，我餓了。

A：我也是。我知道一間很棒的義大利餐廳。

B：那太好了，我們走吧。

Unit 7 ★ 帶到桌子

你一定會用的句型  2-34

1

I would like a nonsmoking table for <u>two</u>.
我想要非吸菸區的兩個位子。

I would like to try it.
我想試試看這個。

I would like to play with you.
我想和你一起玩。

❖❖❖ 替換看看 ❖❖❖

five 五	six 六
three 三	ten 十
eight 八	seven 七

2 We didn't <u>have a reservation</u>.

我們沒有（不）<u>訂位</u>。

We didn't go to the show.
我們沒有去看表演。

We didn't talk to him.
我們沒和他交談。

◆◆◆ 換個單字意思就不一樣囉 ◆◆◆

buy wine 買酒	like the food 喜歡那些餐點
know how to eat it 知道怎麼吃它	order dessert 點甜點
see the price 看到價錢	enjoy the meal 吃得很開心

怎樣都要知道的句子

1. 可以這樣說

■ Welcome to Joe's!
歡迎來到喬的地盤！

■ Do you have a reservation?
你們有預約訂位嗎？

■ I have a reservation.
我有訂位。

■ How many of you, sir?
你們總共幾位呢，先生？

■ Two, please.
兩位，謝謝。

2. 也可以這樣說

■ I'm sorry, but the tables are full.
我很抱歉，但是已經客滿了。

■ How long do we have to wait?
我們要等多久呢？

■ Would you like to sit by the window?
請問你們想要坐窗邊的位子嗎？

■ Smoking or non-smoking?
吸菸還是非吸菸區呢？

■ This way, please.
這邊請。

超常用對話

CD 2-36

A：Good evening, sir. May I help you?

B：Good evening. I would like a non-smoking table for four.

A：Do you have a reservation, sir?

B：No, we don't have a reservation.

A：Then I'm sorry, sir. I'm afraid you have to wait.

A：晚安，先生。我可以為您效勞嗎？

B：晚安。我想要一張四個人的非吸菸桌。

A：您有訂位嗎，先生？

B：不，我們沒有預約訂位。

A：那麼我很抱歉，先生，恐怕您必須等一等了。

Unit 8 ★ 點餐

你一定會用的句型 CD 2-37

1

Do you have <u>spaghetti</u>?
你有義大利麵嗎？

Do you have a pen?
你有筆嗎？

Do you have a nickname?
你有綽號嗎？

 替換看看

hamburgers 漢堡	beef noodles 牛肉麵
pizza 比薩	hot pot 火鍋
curry rice 咖哩飯	Korean BBQ 韓國烤肉

2

<u>This</u> and <u>this</u>, please.

我要這個跟這個。

Tens and twenties, please.

十塊和二十塊,謝謝。

Croissant and milk, please

可頌麵包和牛奶,謝謝。

 ◆◆◆ 換個單字意思就不一樣囉 ◆◆◆

potatoes／veal
馬鈴薯／小牛肉

mutton／lobster
羊肉／龍蝦

prawns／salmon
大蝦／鮭魚

oysters／sirloin
生蠔／沙朗牛排

boiled fish ／
mixed vegetables
白煮魚／綜合鮮蔬

baked chicken ／
garden salad
烤雞／庭園沙拉

怎樣都要知道的句子

1. 可以這樣說  2-38

- Are you ready to order, sir?
  您要點餐了嗎，先生？

- What do you suggest?
  你推薦什麼（餐點）呢？

- What is today's special?
  今日的特餐是？

- This and this, please.
  這個和這個，謝謝。

- I'll have the same, please.
  我也點一樣的，謝謝。

2. 也可以這樣說

- Do you have any local dishes?
  你們有當地特色餐點嗎？

- I'd like some vegetables as an appetizer.
  開胃菜我想要來點蔬菜。

- I'll have fish as the main dish.
  我的主菜要魚。

- Let's try this one.
  我們來試試這個吧。

- How would you like your steak?
  您的牛排要幾分熟？

2-39

A：A chicken salad sandwich and a Coke, please.

B：Sure. Is that all?

A：Uh…do you have muffins?

B：Yes, chocolate and banana.

A：Banana, please.

A：一個雞肉沙拉三明治和可樂。

B：好的。還有什麼嗎？

A：呃…你們有（賣）杯子蛋糕嗎？

B：有的，巧克力和香蕉口味。

A：香蕉，麻煩你。

你 一 定 會 用 的 句 型  2-40

1 Go Dutch, please.
分開付,謝謝。

We will pay separately.
我們要分開付帳。

This is my treat.
這次我請客。

❖❖❖ 替換看看 ❖❖❖

Charge 結帳	Separate checks 個別付帳
Split the bill 分開付	Be my guest this time 這次我請客
This is on me 這次我請客	Let's me foot the bill 讓我出(錢)吧

2 Could I have <u>the bill</u>?

可以給我帳單嗎？

Could we switch seats?

我們可以換位子嗎？

Could you give us some napkins?

你可以給我們一些餐巾紙嗎？

 換個單字意思就不一樣囉

the receipt 收據	the check 帳單
the menu 菜單	another fork 另一支叉子
a small plate 一個小盤子	more bread 更多麵包

怎樣都要知道的句子

1. 可以這樣說   2-41

- Check, please.
  付帳,謝謝。

- Let's go halves.
  我們平均分攤吧。

- Do you accept credit cards?
  你們收信用卡嗎?

- Is it including the service charge?
  有包含服務費嗎?

- Sorry, sir. We don't accept credit cards.
  很抱歉,先生,我們不收信用卡。

2. 也可以這樣說

- I think I have the wrong change.
  我想是找錯錢了。

- Here's your change and receipt, sir.
  這是你的找錢和收據,先生。

- Keep the change.
  不用找了。

- It's delicious.
  東西很好吃。

- Can we have a doggie bag?
  我們可以打包嗎? (回家餵狗)

2-42

A：Can I have the check, please?

B：One moment, sir.

A：Oh, and um…separate checks, please.

B：Separate checks? Of course.

A：Thank you.

A：結帳，麻煩你。

B：稍等一下，先生。

A：噢，還有我們要分開付。

B：分開嗎？當然。

A：謝謝你。

Unit 10 ★ 購物

1 I'm looking for a T-shirt.
我在找T恤。

I'm looking for a gift for my brother.
我在找要送給我哥哥（弟弟）的禮物。

I'm looking for something to match this skirt.
我在找件可以搭配這件裙子的。

◆◆◆ 替換看看 ◆◆◆

jacket 夾克	dress 洋裝
polo shirt 運動衫	dress shirt 襯衫
casual shirt 休閒衫	pullover 套衫

2

I want the <u>red</u> ones.
我要紅色的。

I want a car.
我想要一輛車。

I want some popcorn.
我要買一些爆玉米花。

 換個單字意思就不一樣囉 ◆◆◆

yellow 黃色	gray 灰色	orange 橘色	red 紅色
pink 粉紅色	white 白色	black 黑色	brown 咖啡色
beige 米黃色	blue 藍色	green 綠色	purple 紫色

179

怎樣都要知道的句子

2-44

1. 可以這樣說

- Won't you go shopping with me?
  你不和我一起去購物嗎？

- What are you looking for?
  你在找什麼？

- I'm looking for boots.
  我在找靴子。

- I know a good store.
  我知道一間很棒的店。

- I'm just looking.
  我只是隨意看看。

2. 也可以這樣說

- Why don't you try it on?
  你何不試穿看看？

- How does it fit?
  合身嗎？

- This is nice!
  這很不賴耶！

- What is this made of?
  這是用什麼做的？

- Is this washable?
  這個可以洗嗎？

A：This is a beautiful hat! I want to buy it.

B：Do you wear hats a lot?

A：Yes, I do.

B：Then buy it. I want to buy one, too.

A：這帽子真漂亮！我想把它買下來。

B：你常常戴帽子嗎？

A：是啊。

B：那麼就買吧。我也想買一頂。

你一定會用的句型  2-46

1

Do you have <u>a larger size</u>?
有<u>大一點的尺寸</u>嗎？

Do you have a bigger one?
有大一點的嗎

Do you have cheaper ones?
有便宜一點的嗎？

 替換看看

a medium 中碼	an extra-large 特大
a smaller size 小一點	an extra small 特小
another color 另一個顏色	blue ones 藍色的

2 How much are these <u>heels</u>?

這雙高跟鞋多少錢？

How much is this large bag?

這個大包包要多少錢？

How much is that computer?

那台電腦要多少錢？

 換個單字意思就不一樣囉

sneakers 帆布運動鞋	pumps 氣墊鞋
dress shoes 女用搭配裙子的鞋子	mules 拖鞋
boots 靴子	sandals 涼鞋

怎樣都要知道的句子

1. 可以這樣說　2-47

- This is the right size for you.
  這的尺寸對你來說剛剛好。

- You look good in sweaters.
  你穿毛衣很好看。

- That's not your style.
  那種類型不適合你。

- Red is much better.
  紅色好看多了。

- I think I'll take it.
  我想我就買了它吧。

2. 也可以這樣說

- It's too much for me.
  這對我來說太貴了。

- Can you give me a discount?
  可以幫我打個折嗎？

- Does the price include tax?
  這個價錢有含稅嗎？

- I'll pay in cash.
  我付現金。

- Do you want this wrapped as a gift?
  您這個要包成禮物嗎？

184

2-48

A：I'm looking for heels.

B：What size are you looking for?

A：7, please.

B：How about these?

A：Oh, I like these. How much are these heels?

B：Fifteen dollars.

A：我在找高跟鞋。

B：您在找什麼樣尺寸的呢？

A：7號，謝謝。

B：那麼這些如何？

A：噢，我喜歡這雙，這雙要多少錢？

B：十五塊美金。

Unit **12** ★ 觀光服務站

1

I'd like <u>a round-trip ticket</u>.
我想要一張來回票。

I'd like to see the circus.
我想要去看馬戲團。

I'd like a donut, please.
我想要一個甜甜圈，謝謝。

 替換看看

a one-way ticket 一張單程票	a window seat 一個靠窗的座位
an aisle seat 一個靠走道的坐位	a city map 一張城市地圖
to get a taxi 叫輛計程車	coupon tickets 回數券

2 <u>One-way</u> or <u>round-trip</u>?
單程票還是來回票？

Tea or coffee?
茶還是咖啡？

Chocolate or vanilla?
巧克力還是香草？

 換個單字意思就不一樣囉

Smoking／nonsmoking **吸菸／非吸菸**	Aisle／window seat **走道／靠窗座位**
Local train／express train **普通車／特快車**	Airmail／surface mail **航空信／平信**
Business class／economy class **商務艙／經濟艙**	Today／tomorrow **今天／明天**

怎樣都要知道的句子

1. 可以這樣說 2-50

- Please tell me a place of interest.
  請告訴我一個有趣的地方。

- How much time do you have?
  你有多少時間？

- Where have you been?
  你去過哪些地方了？

- You should visit Taipei 101.
  你應該去一趟台北101。

- It's famous for its beautiful scenery.
  它是因為它美麗的風景而聞名。

2. 也可以這樣說

- I'd like to book a flight.
  我想要訂機票。

- Which night market do you recommend?
  你推薦哪一個夜市呢？

- The National Palace is a must-see in Taipei.
  故宮博物院是台北必去的一個景點。

- Any suggestions?
  有什麼建議嗎？

- Don't forget about the art museum.
  別忘了美術館喔。

CD 2-51

A：I'd like a city map, please.

B：Sure. Are you here on vacation?

A：Yes, I am. But I don't know where to go next. Any suggestions?

B：I think you should visit the National Palace.

A：OK. I hope it's not too far away from here.

A：我想要一張城市地圖。

B：好的。你是來這裡度假的嗎？

A：是啊，但我不曉得接下來要去哪裡。有什麼建議嗎？

B：我認為你該去一下故宮。

A：好啊。希望那裡沒有離這裡太遠。

Unit 13 ★ 遊覽

1 It's <u>wonderful</u>.
那真是太美好了。

It was unforgettable.
那真是令人難忘。

That was impressive.
那真是令人印象深刻。

◆◆◆ 替換看看 ◆◆◆

amazing 太驚人了	unbelievable 令人難以置信
extraordinary 太出色了	stunning 太令人震驚了
great 太棒了	worth the ticket 值回票價

2 How do you like <u>the view</u>?

你喜歡這景色嗎？

How did you find this place?

你是怎麼找到這地方的？

How do you know?

你怎麼知道？

 換個單字意思就不一樣囉

the locals 當地人	the traditional food 傳統食物
the museum 博物館	this place 這地方
Taiwan 台灣	the city 這城市

怎樣都要知道的句子

1. 可以這樣說  2-53

- I'll show you around town today.
  今天我會帶你在鎮上四處看看。

- Where would you like to go?
  你想要去哪裡呢？

- I'd like to go to the art gallery.
  我想要去畫廊。

- What are you interested in?
  你對什麼感興趣呢？

- I'm interested in Japanese history.
  我對日本歷史有興趣。

2. 也可以這樣說

- What a wonder view!
  好棒的景色啊！

- Could you take a picture of us?
  可以麻煩你幫我們照張相嗎？

- Say cheese.
  笑一個。

- We need to get back here by six o'clock.
  我們得在六點時回到這裡。

- Are we ready to go?
  我們準備好要出發了嗎？

2-54

A：This is my first visit to Japan.

B：Where would you like to go?

A：I'd like to visit Kyoto.

B：Kyoto? Why?

A：It's wonderful. It's a very old city, and I'm interested in Japanese history.

B：I see.

A：這是我第一次去日本。

B：你想要去哪裡呢？

A：我想要去京都。

B：京都？為什麼？

A：它很棒！它是很古老的城市，而我對日本歷史很有興趣。

B：我了解了。

Unit 14. 買票

你一定會用的句型  2-55

1

How many <u>tickets</u> do you need?
你需要幾張票呢？

How many people are there?
那邊有幾個人？

How many kids do you have?
你有幾個小孩？

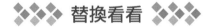 替換看看

maps 地圖	adult tickets 成人票
children's tickets 兒童票	one-way tickets 單程票
coupons 回數券	round-trip tickets 來回票

2

<u>Two adults</u>, please.
<u>兩個大人</u>，謝謝。

Latte, please.
拿鐵，謝謝。

Hold on, please.
請稍等一下。

 換個單字意思就不一樣囉

Three tickets
三張票

Four children's tickets
四張兒童票

Front seats
前排的座位

Center seats
中間的座位

Express train
特快車

Two tickets for
'*Spider man*'
兩張《蜘蛛人》的票。

怎樣都要知道的句子

1. 可以這樣說  2-56

- I'd like to see a puppet show.
  我想要去看布偶戲。

- What time does the show begin?
  表演幾點開始呢？

- Which ticket do you want?
  你想要哪一種票？

- Two C seats, please.
  兩張C座位，謝謝。

- Is there a matinee today?
  今天有馬丁尼嗎？

2. 也可以這樣說

- Do you have any standing room?
  還有站票嗎？

- I'd like two seats for the orchestra.
  我要兩個這交響樂團音樂會的座位。

  Please choose your seats.
- 請選擇您的座位。

  May I see the seating chart, please?
- 可以讓我看一下座位表嗎？

  I'm sorry. It's sold out.
- 我很抱歉，票都賣完了。

 2-57

A：Good morning.

B：Good morning. How can I help you?

A：Three tickets, please. I want a good seat.

B：Here you are.

C：Hurry! The movie is starting.

A：早安。

B：早安。我能為您做什麼嗎？

A：三張票，謝謝。我要好位子喔。

B：請。

C：快點！電影要開始了。

Note

Chapter 5 一路通的交通

Unit 1 ★ 問路

你一定會用的句型  2-58

1

Where is <u>the post office</u>?
<u>郵局</u>在哪裡？

Where is my car?
我的車在哪裡？

Where are your children?
你的孩子們在哪裡？

◆◆◆ 替換看看 ◆◆◆

Central Park 中央公園	the nearest subway station 最近的地鐵站
Hyatt Hotel 君悅飯店	parking lot 停車場
the outlet market 特賣會場	the art museum 美術館

2 How do I get to <u>the airport</u>?
我要如何到機場去呢？

How do I start the car?
我要如何啓動車子？

How do you spell that?
那個字要怎麼拼啊？

 換個單字意思就不一樣囉

the train station 火車站	City Hall 市政府
Meiji Palace 明治神宮	Sienna 西亞那
the Grand Canyon 大峽谷	the beach 海灘

怎樣都要知道的句子

1. 可以這樣說  2-59

- Excuse me!
  不好意思！

- Where's the train station?
  火車站在哪裡？

- Where are you going?
  你要去哪裡？

- Please show me where we are.
  請告訴我我現在的所在位置。

- Is it far to the airport?
  那兒離機場很遠嗎？

2. 也可以這樣說

- Go straight.
  直走。

- Turn left at the second corner.
  第二個路口左轉。

- It's on your left.
  它就在你的左手邊。

- You can't miss it.
  你不可能找不到的。

- Keep walking for three blocks.
  繼續走，走過三個路口。

2-60

A：Excuse me. I'm lost. Can you help me?

B：Sure. Where do you want to go?

A：Taipei Station.

B：OK. Keep walking and turn left at the next corner. It's on the right.

A：Thank you.

B：You're welcome.

A：不好意思，我迷路了，你可以幫幫我嗎？

B：當然可以。你想要去哪裡？

A：台北車站。

B：好，繼續走，在下一個路口左轉。它就在右手邊。

A：謝謝你。

B：不客氣。

Unit 2 ★ 怎麼坐車還有租車呢？

1

Let's go by <u>bus</u>.
我們搭<u>公車</u>去吧。

Let's finish the page.
我們把這頁看完吧。

Let's try again.
我們再試一次看看。

◆◆◆ 替換看看 ◆◆◆

car 汽車	MRT 捷運
train 電車	subway 地鐵
bus 公車	taxi 計程車

2 Do you have any <u>compact</u> cars?
請問你們有<u>小型</u>車嗎？

Do you have the number?
你有電話號碼嗎？

Do you have a job?
你有工作嗎？

 換個單字意思就不一樣囉

economy 省油的	mid-sized 中型的
full-sized 全套的	Japanese 日本的
4-door 四門的	automatic 自排的

怎樣都要知道的句子

1. 可以這樣説  2-62

- Where are you going?
  你要去哪裡？

- How can I get to Taipei Station？
  我要如何才能到達台北總站呢？

- Which line should I take to go to down town?
  我要搭哪一線才能到市中心呢？

- Take the blue line. It's an express train.
  搭藍線，那是特快車。

- That's the nearest stop.
  那是最接近的停靠站了。

2. 也可以這樣説

- Where can I buy a ticket?
  我在哪裡可以買到票呢？

- I'm going to Central Park.
  我準備要去中央公園。

- How much is it to Central Park?
  到中央公園要多少錢？

- It's sixty dollars.
  要六十元。

- A ticket to West 8th Street, Please.
  一張到第八西街的票，謝謝。

超常用對話

CD 2-63

A：What time will the bus leave?

B：It leaves at four.

A：Then we have half an hour to wait. Shall we buy something to drink?

B：Good idea.

A：巴士什麼時候會開？

B：四點會開。

A：那我們還有半小時要等。 我們去買個東西喝好嗎？

B：好主意。

Unit 3 ★ 電車

你一定會用的句型  2-64

1

Which <u>line</u> should we <u>take</u>?
我們該坐哪一線？

Which one will you choose?
你會選擇哪一樣？

Which way do you want to go?
你想要走哪個方向？

◆◆◆ 替換看看 ◆◆◆

platform／go to 月台／去	path ／ take 路／走
car ／get on 車廂／上車	stop ／get off 站／下車
way ／ go 方向／去	seat ／ take 座位／坐

2 What's the <u>departure time</u>?
<u>出發時間</u>是？

What is the reason?
為了什麼原因？

What is the matter?
怎麼了？

 換個單字意思就不一樣囉 ❖❖❖

arrival time 抵達時間	best route 最佳路線
difference 差別	speed limit 速限
next stop 下一站	terminal station 終點站

怎樣都要知道的句子

1. 可以這樣說  2-65

- Where's the train for London?
  往倫敦的火車在哪裡？

- Go down(up) the stairs.
  往樓下（上）走。

- Take the train with green stripes.
  搭乘有綠色條紋的那班火車。

- It's on the 4th platform.
  在第四月台。

- You need to change trains here.
  你得在這裡換車。

2. 也可以這樣說

- What's the next station?
  下一站是？

- It's the terminal station.
  是終點站。

- Where do you get off?
  你在哪裡下車啊？

- Don't sit on the priority seats.
  不要坐在博愛座上。

- Excuse me. This is my seat.
  不好意思，這是我的座位。

超常用對話

CD 2-66

A：Excuse me, which train goes
to London?

B：That orange one over there.

A：I see. Thank you.

B：You're welcome.

A：不好意思，請問哪一班車
是到倫敦的？

B：那邊那一輛橘色的。

A：我知道了，謝謝你。

B：不客氣。

Unit 4 ★ 地鐵

你一定會用的句型  2-67

1

Where is the <u>subway station</u>?
地鐵站在哪裡？

Where are our bags?
我們的包包在哪裡？

Where is it located?
它位在哪裡？

◆◆◆ 替換看看 ◆◆◆

entrance 入口	exit 出口
ticket machine 購票機	fare adjustment office 票價調整處
information desk 詢問處	box office 購票處

2 You have to change to <u>the red</u> line.
你必須轉搭紅線。

We have to cook dinner.
我們得做晚飯了。

I have to work.
我得工作。

 換個單字意思就不一樣囉

Danshui 淡水	Xindian 新店
Zhonghe 中和	Muzha 木柵
Ginza 銀座	Marunouchi 丸之內

怎樣都要知道的句子

1. 可以這樣說  2-68

- Where's the nearest subway station?
  最近的地鐵站在哪裡？

- Does this subway go to Central Park?
  這班地鐵有到中央公園嗎？

- Where do I transfer?
  我要在哪裡轉車？

- The exit is on the right.
  出口在右邊。

- Take the next train .
  搭下一班車。

2. 也可以這樣說

- How many stops to Gig Garden?
  還要過幾站才會到吉格花園？

- Can I have a subway map?
  可以給我一張地鐵圖嗎？

- How late does subway run?
  地鐵行駛到多晚呢？

- Is this a local train?
  這是普通車嗎？

- Which exit should I take to the SEA hotel?
  我要走哪一個出口才會到SEA飯店呢？

2-69

A：Excuse me. Which subway should I take to Green Road?

B：Go to platform 2 and take the red line.

A：How many stops are there from here to Green Road?

B：5 stops.

A：不好意思，我應該要搭哪一班車才能到格林路呢？

B：到第二月台，然後搭紅線。

A：從這裡到格林路有幾站呢？

B：五站。

Unit 5 ★ 公車

1

Where can I catch a/an <u>No.33</u> bus?
我在哪裡可以搭到33號公車呢？

Where can I get my baggage?
我可以在哪裡拿我的行李呢？

Where can I buy some shoes?
我可以在哪裡買鞋呢？

◆◆◆ 替換看看 ◆◆◆

double-decker 雙層的	sight-seeing 觀光
airport 機場	No.226 226號
shuttle 接駁車	community 社區公車

2 Does this bus stop at <u>Hight Street</u>?

這班公車有停海特街嗎？

Does this train go to Daly City?

這班火車有到達利市嗎？

Does this price include tax?

這個價錢有含稅嗎？

 換個單字意思就不一樣囉 ◆◆◆

Balboa Park 巴爾波亞公園	National Taiwan University 國立台灣大學
the zoo 動物園	downtown 市中心
Geary Street 基利街	NTU hospital 臺大醫院

怎樣都要知道的句子

1. 可以這樣説

■ Where can I get on a bus to the airport?
我可以在哪裡搭公車到機場去呢？

■ Is this to the Zhongxiaofuxing intersection?
這是往忠孝復興路口的嗎？

■ I'll ask the driver for you.
我幫你問一下司機。

■ There are four more stops.
還有四站。

■ Don't forget your stuff.
別忘了你的東西。

2. 也可以這樣説

■ Don't sit in the priority seats, please.
請不要坐在博愛座上。

■ What's the next stop?
下一站是什麼？

■ Am I on the right bus?
我搭對車了嗎？

■ I think you took the wrong bus.
我想你搭錯車了。

■ Get off at next stop and take No.311.
在下一站下車，然後改搭311號。

CD 2-72

A：Excuse me, sir. What's the next stop?

B：It's the National Taiwan University.

A：Then...does this bus stop at Taipei Main Station?

B：I don't think so. I think you took the wrong bus.

A：Oh, no!

A：先生，不好意思，請問下一站是？

B：是國立台灣大學。

A：那...這輛車有停台北火車站嗎？

B：恐怕沒有，我想你搭錯公車了。

A：喔，不！

Unit 6 ★ 計程車

你一定會用的句型  2-73

1

Please take me to <u>the airport</u>.
請帶我去機場。

Please take me to the emergency room.
請帶我去急診室。

Please take me to this place.
請到我去這個地方。

◆◆◆ 替換看看 ◆◆◆

the hospital 醫院	the theater 劇院
the police station 警察局	the Grand Hotel 圓山飯店
the harbor 港口	the church 教堂

2 We must <u>go</u> now.
我們現在得走了。

We must be there soon.
我們得火速到達那裡。

We must ask him.
我們得問問他。

◆◆◆ 換個單字意思就不一樣囉 ◆◆◆

talk
談談

leave
離開

hurry
快點

stop
停下來

turn
轉彎

pull over
靠邊停

怎樣都要知道的句子

1. 可以這樣説  2-74

- Where can I get a taxi?
  我在哪裡可以搭到計程車？

- Where's the taxi stand?
  計程車站在哪裡？

- Please take me to this address.
  請帶我到這個地址去。

- Available taxis have a red light.
  可搭乘的計程車會有個紅色的燈。

- To Macy's, please.
  麻煩到梅西百貨公司。

2. 也可以這樣説

- How much?
  多少錢？

- Keep the change.
  不用找了。

- Drive faster, please.
  請開快一點。

- I'm in a hurry.
  我在趕時間。

- Can we get there in ten minutes?
  我們可以在十分鐘內到那裡嗎？

2-75

A：Where to, sir?

B：To the airport, please.

A：OK, sir.

B：Drive faster, please. We must get there before 10:00.

A：No problem, sir.

A：到哪裡呢，先生？

B：麻煩到機場。

A：好的，先生。

B：麻煩你開快一點，我們在十點以前一定要到達那裡。

A：沒問題，先生。

Unit **1** ★ 緊急應變

你一定會用的句型  2-76

1
I lost my <u>passport</u>.
我遺失了我的護照。

I heard it wrong.
我聽錯了。

I knew it.
那我知道。

◆◆◆ 替換看看 ◆◆◆

credit card 信用卡	keys 鑰匙	camera 照相機	luggage 行李
flight ticket 飛機票	necklace 項鏈	watch 手錶	glasses 眼鏡
wallet 皮夾	i-Pod i-Pod		

2

I left it <u>on the bus</u>.

我把它忘在公車上了。

I locked myself out of the car.

我把自己鎖在車外了。

I took the train home.

我是搭火車回家的。

◆◆◆ 換個單字意思就不一樣囉 ◆◆◆

on the train 在火車上	on the table 在桌上
on the taxi 在計程車裡	in the hotel 在飯店裡
in the room 101 在101房裡	at the cashier 在收銀台上

怎樣都要知道的句子

1. 可以這樣說

- Watch out!
  小心！

- Hold it! Stop!
  不要動！停下來！

- What happened?
  發生什麼事了？

- Shall I call an ambulance?
  要不要我叫救護車？

- Don't worry! It'll be OK.
  別擔心，一切都會沒事的。

2. 也可以這樣說

- Catch him!
  抓住他！

- Freeze! Calm down!
  不要動！冷靜點！

- I'll call the police!
  我打電話叫警察！

- A theft report, pease.
  我要通報一則竊案。

- Don't touch anything!
  不要動任何東西！

2-78

A：Oh no, I think I lost my passport!

B：Calm down, Julia. Are you sure?

A：Yes! I can't find it! Maybe I left it in the hotel room.

B：Then let's call the hotel right now.

A：Oh, I hope it's there.

A：喔，不，我想我把護照給弄丟了！

B：冷靜點，茱莉亞。妳確定嗎？

A：我確定！我找不到！也許我把它忘在飯店房間裡了。

B：那麼我們現在就打電話給飯店。

A：噢，我希望是在那裡。

Unit 2 ★ 生病了

你一定會用的句型  2-79

1

I have <u>a stomachache</u>.
我肚子痛。

My mother has a cold.
我媽媽感冒了。

His wife had a baby.
他太太懷孕了。

◆◆◆ 替換看看 ◆◆◆

a headache 頭痛	a runny nose 流鼻涕	a backache 背痛	a toothache 牙痛
the flu 感冒	a fever 發燒	a cough 咳嗽	a sore throat 喉嚨痛
food poisoning 食物中毒	diarrhea 腹瀉		

2

My <u>head</u> hurt(s).
我<u>頭</u>痛。

My stomach hurts.
我胃痛。

She rocks!
她很酷耶！

 換個單字意思就不一樣囉

tummy	foot／feet	back	wrist
肚子	腳	背	手腕

ear	lower back	arm	throat
耳朵	下背部	手臂	喉嚨

neck	knee(s)	leg	thumb
脖子	膝蓋	腿	拇指

怎樣都要知道的句子

1. 可以這樣說  2-80

- You look so pale.
  你的臉色好蒼白。

- I have a cough.
  我咳嗽。

- I feel dizzy.
  我頭暈。

- I got hurt.
  我受傷了。

- You had better see a doctor.
  你最好去看個醫生。

2. 也可以這樣說

- Do you feel any discomfort?
  你有覺得什麼不舒服的嗎？

- Open your mouth.
  張開嘴巴。

- I'll write you a prescription.
  我給你開一張處方籤。

- Take this three times daily.
  一天吃三次。

- Take this after meals.
  這個要飯後再服用。

超常用對話

 2-81

A：Mary, you look tired today.

B：Yeah, and I have a headache.

A：Why do you have a headache?

B：Because I drank too much last night.

A：That's too bad.

A：瑪麗，妳今天看起來很累呢。

B：是啊，而且我頭痛。

A：為什麼妳會頭痛呢？

B：因為我昨天晚上酒喝太多了。

A：那還真是糟糕。

I good 英語 02

情境會話 × 萬用好句 × 生活單字

遊學、留學生活英語
一個月就出發去歐美

25K+2CD

發行人 ●	林德勝
著者 ●	李洋
出版發行 ●	山田社文化事業有限公司
	臺北市大安區安和路一段112巷17號7樓
	電話 02-2755-7622
	傳真 02-2700-1887
郵政劃撥 ●	19867160號　大原文化事業有限公司
網路購書 ●	日語英語學習網　http://www. daybooks. com. tw
總經銷 ●	聯合發行股份有限公司
	新北市新店區寶橋路235巷6弄6號2樓
	電話 02-2917-8022
	傳真 02-2915-6275
印刷 ●	上鎰數位科技印刷有限公司
法律顧問 ●	林長振法律事務所　林長振律師
初版 ●	2015年8月
定價 ●	新台幣310元
ISBN ●	978-986-246-333-8